Ciel
in All Directions

SOPHIE LABELLE

TRANSLATED BY ANDREA ZANIN

Second Story Press

Library and Archives Canada Cataloguing in Publication

Title: Ciel in all directions / Sophie Labelle ; translated by Andrea Zanin.
Other titles: Ciel. Dans toutes les directions. English
Names: Labelle, Sophie, 1988- author. | Zanin, Andrea, translator.
Description: Translation of: Ciel. Dans toutes les directions
Identifiers: Canadiana (print) 20210140577 | Canadiana (ebook) 20210140585
 | ISBN 9781772602036 (softcover) | ISBN 9781772602043 (EPUB)
Classification: LCC PS8623.A23235 C54313 2021 | DDC jC843/.6—dc23

Cover illustration by Sophie Labelle

All emojis designed by OpenMoji—the open-source emoji and icon project.
License: CC BY-SA 4.0

Printed and bound in Canada

*Second Story Press gratefully acknowledges the support of the Ontario Arts Council
and the Canada Council for the Arts for our publishing program. We acknowledge
the financial support of the Government of Canada through the Canada Book Fund.*

 **ONTARIO ARTS COUNCIL
CONSEIL DES ARTS DE L'ONTARIO**

 Canada Council   Conseil des Arts
for the Arts   du Canada

Funded by the Government of Canada
Financé par le gouvernement du Canada    Canadä

Published by
Second Story Press
20 Maud Street, Suite 401
Toronto, Ontario, Canada
M5V 2M5
www.secondstorypress.ca

 MIX
Paper from
responsible sources
FSC® C103567

1

My Gang of Devils

"Wow, your hair is way cool, Ciel!"

I smile at Frank before sitting at the desk just behind his. I'm flattered he noticed my new haircut, even though it wasn't hard to notice, considering the change is pretty drastic. I'd gotten tired of my blunt cut; it was too sensible for my liking. I'd been thinking about it for a few days, and last night, I finally went to the hairdresser. I asked him to shave the sides and keep a good length on top and for my bangs. Because I was feeling daring, I also got him to dye my light brown hair to a blonde so pale it's almost white. I like the contrast with the very classic black blouse I'm wearing today!

The bell rings, and the classroom noise level drops. Nathaniel Brazeau, our science and technology teacher, takes his place in front of us with a pile of documents.

"All right, you gang of devils, we're starting, so I don't want to see a single one of you on your phone! As I announced last class, this morning you're going to start your personal projects for the fall."

Mr. Brazeau (that's what we have to call him, even if it makes him seem older) has a pretty unusual style that's different from the other adults at my high school: he has shoulder-length black hair, he only wears band T-shirts for punk music groups from the early 2000s, and he starts every class with a heartfelt "all right, my gang of devils." Rumor has it that he's a guitarist in his spare time and that he spent last summer on tour with his band all over Québec. He's not my kind of guy, I have to say. He's very cool and he gives off good energy, but I find him a little too keyed-up. Anyway, most of the girls and some of the guys look at him with stars in their eyes. Like Stephie, my best friend (and Frank's girlfriend!), who doesn't have him as a teacher but insists on walking me to class every time I have a period with him just so she can look at him from the hallway. She's terrible.

It bothers me a bit that we're not always together in all our classes like we were in elementary school. She and I have been friends since fourth grade. Stephie's a real go-getter, the kind who's not afraid to raise her hand and who likes to get into arguments with teachers. As for me, just the idea of speaking up in class makes me break out in a cold sweat. That's why people are often surprised to learn I have a YouTube channel where I post little funny videos. But talking in front of Virgil, my little brother (who acts as my cameraman), is a very different thing from talking in front of a bunch of first-year high school students.

It would be easy to simplify the story of my friendship with Stephie by saying we're both transgender. Of course that brings us closer, the fact that the doctors and our parents made a mistake about our genders at birth, and proclaimed us both boys without asking our opinion, so we both had to convince everyone that wasn't the case.... However, unlike Stephie, I'm not exactly a girl. I'm not exactly a boy, either. Instead, I consider myself between the two. I use the pronoun "they." It can be a little confusing for people. In the hallway this morning, someone wanted to know what I was again. So I answered in a hollow voice: "I am your worst nightmare."

And I think that pretty much sums up the situation. I have to say, it also makes things complicated at school. When I started high school, the teachers only had my birth name on their official lists, Alessandro Sousa. Because I wasn't comfortable being called that, I screwed up my courage and asked them to change it to

Alessandra. That's the compromise I found. But I prefer when people call me Ciel; that's my online handle, and it's what the people I trust call me.

My gaze falls on Frank, who's listening to our teacher attentively. We're not the best of friends, but he's the person I know best in this class, since he went to the same elementary school as me and Stephie. Sometimes I can't stand him, especially when he starts talking about soccer, but I know he's a good guy at heart. The seat next to him is always saved for Viktor, his best friend. I keep a safe distance from Viktor to avoid having to listen to his terrible jokes during class. Viktor's not mean, it's just that I can only roll my eyes so far back in their sockets.

As he keeps talking, Mr. Brazeau starts handing out his sheets to the front row of students, who each keep one and pass the rest of the pile back.

"This handout tells you the steps you need to follow to create your personal project. Take good care of it, like it's the apple of your eye. A baby seal will go blind every time one of you loses your copy of this. Imagine a baby seal never being able to see its parents again. Surely you don't want that to happen?"

A few of Mr. Brazeau's fans burst out laughing.

"Overall, your goal for the next three weeks—which takes us to October 18—will be to choose a skill you haven't mastered yet, and do the necessary research so that you can apply it. I'd advise you to keep it simple. I don't want you to learn how to shoot a rocket into space or create your own nuclear power plant. Think about something that interests you and that you can then share with the class, like the basics of coding, making your own soap, or even sewing."

I hear Viktor laugh at the idea of learning how to sew. I sigh, feeling discouraged.

Mr. Brazeau continues, "You need to use at least three sources. That can be a website, a book, a qualified person, or a member of your family. If you're not sure about your sources, you can come see me or send me an email. Your job, between now and the end of class today, is to figure out what subject your personal project will be about and come to me so I can approve your idea. You can use the computers and the library, if you want. Any questions?"

Every time Mr. Brazeau asks if there are any questions, it's as if he's just announced that the school was imposing a mandatory uniform or something. Everyone seems to panic and start talking all at once.

"One at a time! Raise your hands, please! Yes?"

A girl in a green top speaks up. "Can my project be cooking a recipe?"

"Don't submit your ideas yet, come see me during the—"

"Yeah, but what if it's a complicated recipe, like a pastry?"

"I'll say it again. I'm not going to approve projects in front of the class, come see me in a bit. Does anyone have a question that's not about your project idea?"

All of a sudden, there are only a few hands up. Frank, who kept his in the air, sounds a bit stressed out when he asks, "Can we do this in a team?"

The whole class turns toward Mr. Brazeau.

"Unfortunately, as the name says, the project is personal. It has to be done individually. In any case, you'll have group projects in other subjects."

A weak wave of protest rises, but Mr. Brazeau stops it short by ordering us to read the instructions in silence.

I flip through the pages distractedly. There must be some way to work my YouTube channel into the project…I bought a new camera just recently and I still don't know how to use all its features. My personal project could be to read the instruction manual, which I barely looked at because the technical language was so complicated. But that would be incredibly dull….

The students start to get up to go to Mr. Brazeau's office or to the computers. I take the opportunity to discreetly take my phone out of my bag and text Stephie. I send her a photo of Frank's back, with the teacher in the background. A second later, my phone vibrates.

My two faves!

We have a personal project to do, we have to learn something we don't know yet.

Wow, that's specific...

I know!

Your project could be about Liam, that way you'd have a reason to spend time with him!

???

Liam is another first-year student, and he's also trans. Because he and I get along well, Stephie's got it into her head that we should date. Oh, didn't I mention? She can be annoying sometimes.

Still, it's true that Liam's awesome. He's very sensitive, artistic, and brilliant. Pretty good-looking, I'd say, even if athletes aren't really my type, usually. He's a member of the Québec junior swim team, so he spends his time training. Quite the opposite of me, I almost never do any exercise!

Then I hear Mr. Brazeau say my name. "Alessandra! I hope you're using your phone for your project?"

♥ ♥ ♥

When science class is over, I head to the locker I share with Stephie, right near the student entrance. She comes up behind me, skipping like a child, and with a big smile says, "That haircut looks so good on you!"

"Thanks, thanks. How are you?"

"My heart is broken to pieces. You know my English teacher, the one I really liked?"

"Uh-oh. 'Liked' in the past tense."

"For real! He gave me a B on my last test."

"Congrats!"

"Congrats? It's going to bring down my average!"

Stephie has always been at the top of her classes. Which makes sense, she's extremely intelligent. Anyway, she's a lot smarter than me.

"A B is already higher than the average."

"It's frustrating! And it's his fault, too. He gave a really bad explanation about what the test was on."

"You'll bounce back. I'm sure you'll get bonus points in other tests or something."

Stephie has surely noticed I'm bored with the

subject, because she asks, "So, did you end up finding an idea for your personal project?"

"I went to see the teacher to tell him I wanted to do something related to my YouTube channel, but he said that was too vague. So I need to find an idea by next week."

"Hmm. You could...I dunno...learn how to add special effects?"

"I have no idea how to make computer-generated explosions!"

"It can't be that complicated. I'm sure there are apps on your phone for that."

While she puts away her books and pulls out her lunch box, I ask her, "How was your play yesterday?"

"Well, first of all, it wasn't a play, but rather an ex-perimental ballet. And second, it was...strange. I'm not sure I liked it."

"Why not?"

"Because I didn't really get it. At one point, it looked like people were coming out of the stomach of one of the dancers. I think we were also supposed to see some of them as animals. Oh, and the music was scary."

"Wow! That doesn't make much sense."

"Well, my mother loved it, anyway. You would sure-ly have hated it. There were lots of strobe lights during the 'birthing.'"

What she's describing does sound like a nightmare for me. I get dizzy every time I'm around bright blinking lights. I decide to change the subject.

"Are we still having lunch at the Gender and Sexuality Alliance meeting?"

"For sure. I promised Zoe and Samira I'd be there."

The Gender and Sexuality Alliance is the school's lesbian, gay, bisexual, and trans committee. Everyone is welcome. It's not a particularly fun group, but we're lucky we have it. I'm guessing not very many schools have associations like it, where students like me or Stephie can get involved without worrying about discrimination. Surprised, I say, "Samira will be there? That's new."

"Yup. I just learned her dad is a trans woman, and I told her it would be cool if she came. Do you know if your gorgeous Liam will be there too?"

"He's not *my* Liam. And I'm not sure. He's leaving tonight for his swim competition in Acadie, so he might decide to go rest at home instead."

"I don't know how he finds the time to go home to eat! We've got barely an hour and a half for lunch."

"I told you, he lives right next to the school."

"Oh, right. Anyway, it's handy for your little get-togethers…."

Stephie winks at me as we open the door to the classroom where the Gender and Sexuality Alliance is meeting. I don't have time to respond; I see Liam in his oversized kangaroo sweatshirt, the one he has in four different colors (gray, dark gray, black, dark blue) and that he wears almost every day. We make our way toward him automatically. Stephie smiles. "Hey Liam! Is that spot taken?"

"Hey, you two! Of course, have a seat, I'm not expecting anyone."

My friend makes a shocked face. "Not even us? Honestly!"

"Uh…yeah, sure, I was expecting you."

"I'm teasing you."

I step on Stephie's foot, because she sat down much too close to me, sandwiching me against Liam. She could be a little more subtle.

Liam squints as he looks at me, and then says, "Feels like there's something different about you today…."

I push back a strand of hair coquettishly. "Oh, you noticed?"

"Is it a new top?"

"No! I got a new haircut!"

Liam starts laughing. "I'm teasing you. It looks great!"

"Thanks! I wasn't sure you'd come today, because of your competition."

"I don't really feel like going, to be honest. We're

going to get there around midnight, spend all day tomorrow at the pool, sleep over, and then take the plane back again super early Sunday morning."

"Where do you stay on your trips?"

"Depends. This time, it's a pretty big competition, so we'll be at the hotel, but sometimes we've slept on mattresses in a gym."

Stephie is impressed. "You stay at a hotel! Wow! With room service and breakfast included?"

"Honestly, it's nothing special. My mom makes better breakfasts."

"Yeah, but it's so classy! Me, I'd order ice cream to my room every chance I got. Yum!"

Samira and Zoe show up. They're Stephie's friends who we usually eat with at the cafeteria. They say hello, compliment me on my hair, and pull up chairs to sit near us. Samira turns toward Liam. "I'm not sure we've met!"

"Not officially, but we have the same music, phys ed, and science and tech classes. It's…Samira, right?"

"You've got a good memory!"

"Yeah. My name's Liam."

The room gradually fills up. I recognize a number of people who were at the last meeting, when we discussed the activities we'd like to do throughout the school year. Mael-a's blue hair stands out from the crowd. They're in fourth year and they know my YouTube channel—I'm so glad I finally learned their name! Our eyes meet, and when I realize they're coming over to me, I get shy. We've spoken a few times, Mael-a and I, but I'm always intimidated when older students talk to me.

"Hey, Ciel! I won't bother you long, I just wanted to congratulate you on your last video. By the way, is Bettie Bobbie Barton still getting on your case?"

Bettie Bobbie Barton is a YouTuber who recently posted a video where she makes fun of me and makes racist comments about my Brazilian origins. I responded by making a new video to reply to her attacks.

"Oh my goodness, no! I get the sense she's already bored of me!" I say and shrug my shoulders.

"Is that where it comes from? The name of your channel, *Ciel Is Boring*?"

"Uh...it's *Ciel Is Bored*...."

"I know. It was a joke."

I laugh and turn red. Fourth-year humor is too complicated for me. Mael-a moves on and addresses the group.

"Are you coming to the youth group at the LGBT+ Youth Center next week? It's the second meeting since coming back from summer vacation, but last time almost nobody showed up! We announced it on Facebook, but apparently that wasn't enough."

I answer, "I'm interested! I haven't been since May."

Zoe and Samira shake their heads. I look at Stephie and Liam, who seem to hesitate. Stephie asks, "What day is it? I babysit on Tuesday and Wednesday."

"It's Wednesday night, unfortunately."

Liam jumps in. "I could make it. It's near Beaudry metro station, right?"

Mael-a smiles. "You got it! I'll see you there, then. I'm assisting Armand, who runs it."

Just then, everyone quiets down when they see the Alliance leaders get up and stand in front. Mael-a waves and goes back to sit with the older kids at the back of the room.

Jérôme-Lou, the president of the Alliance, who's always dressed very preppy, opens his mouth to speak but is interrupted right away by someone whistling at him. He winks, and then starts his speech, making big arm movements.

"Ha ha ha. Hello, dear members! I'm honored to open this third meeting of the Gender and Sexuality Alliance. I hope you've had a good week. Ha ha ha. Myself, I had the pleasure of attending an experimental ballet last night, which was in excellent taste and from which I emerged more inspired than ever for this school year. I'll spare you the details, because you really had to be there to understand the powerful message of the show. Ha ha ha."

I poke Stephie with my elbow as I try unsuccessfully to hide my giggling. She rolls her eyes to the ceiling, exasperated.

Jérôme-Lou continues, "Without further ado, let's move on to the main affair, which is to say, preparing for the school elections. As you know, each committee representative is elected in a school-wide vote. That means anyone can run. This year, the election will take place on October 17, in about three weeks. Good luck to anyone who wants to run against me, ha ha ha. You also need to present yourselves with a running mate, who will become the Alliance vice-president if you're elected. I don't want to discourage you, far from it, but the job of president and vice-president are not fun and games. In addition to making sure the Alliance meetings go off without a hitch, the president needs to attend all the school council meetings and run their projects by the student life director. The vice-president, for his part, needs to assist the president in his tasks and make sure he's always well coiffed. Ha ha ha. That's a joke, because Marine, our vice-president, takes care of my hairdo on a fully volunteer basis. But enough with the jokes. It's important for the vice-president to be prepared for any eventuality and ready to take up the president's torch as needed...."

I stop listening, because I find Jérôme-Lou kind of exhausting. Anyway, it's not like this has anything to do with me: there's no way I'd run for office. So, I focus on my lunch. Under my sandwich container, I see a note from my father: "I made this sandwich with all my love (and a little bit of mayonnaise)." Yeah, I know, it's weird that my dad still makes my lunch in high school, but it would break his heart if I asked him to stop.

I realize that Jérôme-Lou has finished his pompous speech when people start chatting again and moving around the room. Stephie puts her hand on my shoulder. "You know what, Ciel? You should run. You'd be a great president!"

"Me?! You've gotta be joking. I have anxiety attacks every time I need to speak up in class. If there's any one of us who should be president, it's you, Ms. Model Student!"

Stephie flips her hair behind her shoulder as if she were in a shampoo commercial. "Oh, you think so? It's true that I'm pretty extraordinary."

Liam jumps in. "Well, I sure would vote for you two if you ran together. You make such a great team!"

Zoe exclaims, "Aw, yes! You're too cute together. Not only would I vote for you, but I ship you!"

Liam, looking confused, asks, "'I ship you?' What does that mean?"

"It's when you think two people go well together. You give a name to the 'ship' by mixing the two names together. Here, for example, we'd have Ciphie. Or maybe Stephel."

"Ha ha! I like Stephel," says Liam.

I give him a look of mock discouragement. Zoe and Samira start debating the best name, while Liam laughs behind them. "Vote Stephel! Stephel for president!"

"Meh! You're not going to convince me like that."

Stephie gives me a squeeze, and proclaims, "Anyway, I don't need an election to know you're the president of my heart."

Samira and Zoe let out an "awww" in chorus, and I realize I'm not out of the woods.

2

Dolores von Tragic Enters the Scene

I let out a long sigh and let myself flop against the back of the sofa. It's Sunday, and it's raining buckets. I try to focus on a comic book Liam lent me, after I admitted I didn't really like reading. He refused to believe me. He said it was just because I hadn't found the right book. I don't know if this is the right one, but I definitely prefer comic books over the novels they make us read at school. They have less text, and they're often a lot funnier.

Yesterday, I spent the day waiting for Stephie and Liam to answer my messages. Stephie was with Frank, and Liam was at his competition, so neither one of them had time to pay attention to me. I had planned to go for a bike ride in the park, but the rain never let up, so instead I watched TV all afternoon with Virgil, my nine-year-old brother. I also had to babysit him at night because my dad went to the movies with Myriam, a teacher who works in the same department as him at Collège Ahuntsic.

To kill time, we started playing one of our favorite games: putting together a diva costume, applying ultra-theatrical makeup, and inventing names and stories for ourselves. After that, we took photos of ourselves in stylized poses. Virgil's character was really funny: Dolores von Tragic, the heir to a major company that sells canned tuna. The photos were so good that I created an Instagram account for the character. Virgil was thrilled because he's a huge fan of the drag queen shows on Netflix, where people, mostly men, dress up as divas and undertake different challenges each week, like musical performances and photo sessions.

This afternoon, I have a Skype date with Eiríkur. At least I'll have some entertainment in my day! Eiríkur is the guy I was dating before he moved back to Iceland with his parents in June. We broke up a little after the school year began, because he found it too hard to do a long-distance relationship. We decided to stay in touch, but since then things have been a little uncomfortable between us.

The whole family is at home, for once. My dad is settled in the living room chair, surrounded by his computer and textbooks. I think he's putting together an exam. He really likes creating them himself. He often complains that students are usually expected to learn all the material by heart, whereas my dad prefers to encourage them to think things through for themselves. He's quite the optimist!

Virgil is on the computer, playing Minecraft online with João, his Brazilian best friend. He's using a headset with a mic, so all I hear are little snippets of animated conversation, half in English and half in Brazilian Portuguese. I notice that he's wearing an old, pale blue tutu I gave him. Just like me, my brother has pretty eclectic tastes in clothing, except that he prefers to dress up only at home. His classmates don't suspect a thing; only João knows, because he sometimes comes over to play here.

Lastly, there's Borki, our dog, who's getting fatter by the day. He's stretched out on the sofa at my feet. I hear him snore and fart once in a while. Ewww!

The sound of the rain against the big living room window makes me sleepy, and I fight it off until the time we agreed on, which finally arrives. I get up and touch Virgil's shoulder. He takes off the headset.

"What?"

"I need the computer, I have a Skype date. I told you about it this morning, remember?"

"Can it wait a bit? We're almost finished our cow prison."

"It's called an enclosure."

"No, no, it's a prison, it's for cow criminals. Can't you use your phone instead? You have the Skype app on it."

"Cow criminals? What kind of game is that? And no, the sound is always horrible on the phone, and the camera shakes."

"If I give you the computer, what will you give me in return?"

"I can trade you my Lunala in Pokémon Moon."

"Huh? I'm the one who gave it to you in the first place!"

"And it was a very bad trade! Lunala is one of the best Pokémons. You should want it back."

Virgil thinks about this, and then says, decisively, "Okay, on the condition we make a video with Dolores von Tragic this week."

"Deal."

He says good-bye to João and logs off his game to give me his seat. My dad looks up from his computer and asks, "Do you want me to go work in the kitchen? You'll have more quiet."

I shrug. I'd prefer if he wasn't there, but at the same time, it's not like Eiríkur and I will be saying anything private to each other.

Still, my dad gathers up his textbooks and shuts his laptop, then kisses me on the top of the head and moves into the kitchen.

I send Eiríkur a message to tell him I'm ready. A second later, he replies that he is too, and we start the call. I see his chubby-cheeked face appear on the screen. He has dark circles under his eyes. He exclaims, "Hey, Ciel! How's it going?"

Oh, I've really missed his Nordic accent!

"Not bad, not bad. You?"

"I was really sick, but I'm feeling better. I missed school the other day."

"Yeah, I think you mentioned!"

We talk about boring stuff for a few minutes, like the rain and the nice weather. There are even some moments of silence as we try to figure out what to say to each other and smile tight smiles. I'm starting to worry we won't be able to make this friendship work.

Suddenly, Eiríkur's face lights up.

"Oh, by the way, I made a friend who's trans! Her name is Solveig. I think you'd get along well with her!"

Why is he telling me about his new friend? Is he trying to make me jealous? I force myself to look interested regardless.

"Oh yeah?"

"Actually, I didn't know she was trans, I found out

on TV. Her parents decided to take her elementary school to court because the teachers insisted on calling her by her old name and using male pronouns."

"Wow, that's awful."

"Yup. But since our high school wanted to avoid trouble, the principal added into the policies that it's forbidden to discriminate against a person for their gender identity. Pretty cool."

"Hmm. I'd like it if there were a rule like that at my high school."

I go quiet for a moment. I'd really like to talk to him about Liam, just to show him that my friendships are changing too, and that life goes on even if he's not here anymore. I chew on the idea for a few seconds, and then drop it. I feel mean for wanting to make him jealous because I'm afraid he'll get over me too quickly.

When we say good-bye after talking for a good half-hour, I feel good. I'm proud that I didn't give in to the temptation of mentioning Liam to Eiríkur. Still, I can't help going to look through his Facebook friends, in case I might come across the profile of the trans girl he spoke about. Not to spy on her, no…. Well, okay, maybe. But just a little. After a few minutes, I give up on my search, feeling ridiculous for getting worked up about it. But I'm still thinking about the inclusion policy at Eiríkur's high school. It would be so great if we had a rule like that at Simonne Monet-Chartrand. Maybe that could even be the topic for my next YouTube video!

I decide to talk about it with Virgil. I push open the door to his room and find him stretched out on his belly on the floor, playing with his electrical circuit-building kit (he has unusual hobbies). Borki, who follows him everywhere, is next to him.

As soon as I walk in, my little brother protests, "You could at least knock before coming in! I have a right to my privacy!"

"Oh, come on. We were still sharing a room three months ago, and you never had a problem with that."

"It's not the same now. I'm entering pre-puberty."

"Oh, excuse me! It's just that I remember the fits you pitched because you didn't want us to have separate bedrooms."

He sighs in irritation. "Well, what do you want? Are you done on the computer?"

"Yes, but I just thought of an excellent video idea. Wanna help me?"

Virgil thinks about it for a few seconds like he wants me to feel bad for entering his room without permission, but he ends up agreeing, as always. He adds, "Dolores von Tragic will have to make a guest appearance."

"Yeah, we'll see."

He sits up and smooths down his tutu, which had

wrinkled underneath him. I bend to scratch Borki behind the ears.

Virgil asks, "Did your hang out go well?"

"Of course, why wouldn't it?"

"Because you and Eiríkur had a fight. You're not together anymore."

"We didn't have a fight. It's just that he lives too far
away now."

"Oh, I see," he answers. He doesn't look convinced.
"So, what are you going to talk about in the video?"

"About how it's important for schools to have a rule
saying that trans people and people with different gender expressions are welcome."

"Okay, that's specific. Where do you want to film it?
We can't go to the park this time."

"No, that's true. Um…in the living room, maybe?"

Virgil gets up, and so does Borki, who's not interested in hanging out alone with the electrical circuits. The
two of them come with me to my room. I grab my new
camera and tripod, which we're going to set up in the
living room, facing the sofa.

Virgil says, "I think it'll work well this way."

"Hmm. I'm not sure. Look, you can see all your
things."

"They're not just my things, Borki's toys are there
too."

We turn the camera to find an angle that won't show the huge mess in the living room, but it's hopeless.

"Maybe if you stand against the wall and we zoom in on your face...."

"That would look weird. Wait...."

I take the equipment and head to the kitchen, with Virgil and Borki on my heels. My dad has abandoned his textbooks on the table and is making dinner, a vegetable stir-fry with rice. We quickly realize that the oil sizzling in the wok is making way too much noise for us to hear anything on a video. I almost want to ask my dad to stop cooking for a minute, but I hold back—I don't think that would be very polite. My dad glances over at us.

"Can I help you? Do you want me in your movie?"

Virgil cracks up. "You, Dad? That would be ridiculous!"

"I could be the dad who does backup dancing while cooking!" He starts whistling and wiggling his hips while stirring the vegetables.

"Thanks for offering," I say, holding back from laughing. "It would get me lots of hits, but we need a quiet place to talk."

We head back to my room, and try to ignore the objects strewn all over the floor and furniture: clothes, my old tap shoes, stuffed animals, board games I haven't played in centuries....

"We could just cover everything with a sheet," Virgil says, exasperated.

I answer sarcastically. "That's a great idea!"

"You think so?"

"No. But it does remind me of a video I saw on YouTube, where a guy filmed himself in front of a neon-colored curtain and then changed the background to show videos and funny pictures."

"Do you want to do that?"

"Why not? It would be cool!"

"It sounds pretty complicated. Wouldn't it be easier to clean up your room instead?"

"That's also a very good idea! You take care of cleaning up, and I'll get online and find out how to do the thing with the curtain. Does that work?"

Sighing, Virgil starts picking my clothes up off the floor.

♥ ♥ ♥

Finding information on the subject turns out to be harder than I'd expected, especially because I don't understand the technical terms. Meanwhile, Virgil has set up a welcoming corner near my lamp. He even went into his room to get our old Disney *Cars* soft chair, which is too small for me now but creates a comical effect when I sit in it.

To reward him for his effort, I agree to have Dolores von Tragic appear in my video. He happily hurries to put on his costume, which includes a red dress with a train, a boa, and a large straw hat. I take care of his makeup: a generous coat of mascara, very pink blush, and lipstick that matches the dress.

Holding my school agenda, which contains the school rules, Dolores von Tragic speaks to the camera. "Oh! You're here! In this cruel and merciless world, it is such a joy to see you behind the screen! Yes, you recognized me. I am Dolores von Tragic, heiress of Tragic Tuna and Salmon, Incorporated, Outremont's preferred provider of canned fish since 1855. It is my pleasure to introduce you to my confidant and stylist, Ciel!"

My little brother hands me my agenda and settles in behind the camera.

"Thank you, Dolores von Tragic," I say as I sit down in the chair, which flattens under my weight. "Hello, everyone! I hope you're doing well. My name is Ciel, and, as you know, I started high school last month. Like most schools in Canada, my high school doesn't have a clear rule prohibiting discrimination against trans people. That makes for some unpleasant situations, like the ones I've spoken about in other videos, such as the lack of gender-neutral bathrooms at my school. Nothing prevents people from using the wrong pronoun or the wrong gender to talk about someone, which can create other problems. That means a teacher is allowed to call a student 'he' even if that really hurts her feelings. If my school adopted a rule against this sort of thing, it would send a clear message to the teachers and to all the students—"

Just then, my dad calls out from the kitchen that dinner is ready. Virgil gets agitated, and I lose my train of thought.

"It would send the message that…uh…that people like us exist…and that…."

I look at Virgil, hoping to find a clue on his face about what I was talking about, but I can't catch his eye under all the mascara. My dad opens the bedroom door. "Virgil, Ciel, dinn—oh! Pardon me!"

"Um…. Well, I'm Ciel, with *Ciel Is Bored*. Subscribe to my channel!"

3

The Joys of Being Shipped

The bell rings, and the students erupt with noise. I gather up my books and leave Mr. Brazeau's class, filled with a pleasant feeling of satisfaction. Before class, I went to see him to submit the topic of my personal project: learning to create special effects in the backgrounds of my videos using a curtain. He was very interested in my proposal and accepted it right away. Some other students haven't been so lucky: Frank, for example, still doesn't have an idea. The teacher gave him until next class to find one, or the teacher will pick one for him. If that happens, it's a good bet it'll be a super boring project!

As I walk down the stairs, I check my cell phone. I have a few more YouTube notifications. Sunday night, I edited my video so that you can't hear my dad calling for us to come to dinner, and I posted it on my channel the next day. My usual subscribers commented on it, including Benoît, a friend who lives in Quebec City who was all excited because he had the same *Cars* soft chair when he was little. He hoped it would become a recurring prop in my videos. There were also a lot of comments about Dolores von Tragic. People seem to have really liked her!

"Dolores von Tragic, you're my idol!!!"

"It's not easy being famous like you, Dolores von Tragic, but please know you have all our support!"

"Dolores von Tragic on *Ciel Is Bored*?! We're playing in the big leagues now!"

"Petition to have more Dolores von Tragic appearances on *Ciel Is Bored*!"

Seeing how popular the character was, last night I recorded a short video on my phone of Dolores von Tragic eating dinner, complaining about having dropped a hot piece of broccoli down her cleavage, with red lipstick smeared all over her chin. I promised myself I would post it soon. It will be great content for Dolores fans!

When I get to my locker, I see Frank deep in discussion with Stephie. She seems really upset. She's waving her arms around so wildly that she nearly smacks me when I get closer. I clear my throat so she knows I'm there.

"Hey! You doing okay?"

"No! It's the end of the world!" Stephie exclaims, sounding hopeless.

She can be so dramatic when she wants to be! Turning her back to Frank, she says to me, as if he weren't there, "This guy, who's supposed to be my boyfriend, thinks it's too much trouble to keep me company while I'm babysitting tonight, even though it's two blocks from his house!"

"I have a soccer game after school!" Frank defends himself.

Stephie turns back toward him, exasperated. "That ends at six-thirty, latest. I'm babysitting until ten o'clock! You have time to shower, change, eat, watch TV with your little sisters, read them a bedtime story, have an unpleasant conversation with your parents about your grade on the last English test, and still come see me for at least half an hour!"

"You think my parents will let me go out after nine? You should know them better than that!"

"Fine, then there's nothing more to say." She slips her arm around my neck and says, in a honeyed voice, "Instead, my best friend will come, and we'll have a romantic evening together. Isn't that right, Ciel?"

"Hmm, I don't know if changing a baby's diaper is all that romantic...."

"Momo is two and a half, he only wears diapers to bed. And I put him to bed around seven o'clock."

"But today is Wednesday, and tonight is when I'm going to the Montréal LGBT+ Center with Liam...."

Stephie takes her arm away and lets out a huge sigh.

"Fine, I understand. Leave me all alone in Momo's parents' huge house to watch Netflix on their brand-new curved-screen TV."

Frank's expression turns interested. "Wait, they have a curved TV? You didn't say that."

Well, look at that. I get the sense that Frank may find a way to go visit Stephie....

The first bell rings, and we part ways to head to our classrooms. Frank has math, while Stephie and I are going to French. On our way to the classroom, we come face to face with Jérôme-Lou and Marine, who are handing out flyers in the hallway.

The president of the Gender and Sexuality Alliance comes toward us, calling out, "The school elections are coming! Vote for Jérôme-Lou, a guy just like you, ha ha ha. Oh! Familiar faces!"

He stops to shake our hands, and then hands us flyers. "Do you already know who you're voting for?"

"We don't even know who wants to run yet!" Stephie answers.

"Yes, but you already know who's going to win! Ha ha ha."

"Ah, yes, of course." Stephie's sarcasm goes ten feet over Jérôme-Lou's head. She looks at the flyer he gave her, which shows a selfie of the two candidates with a filter that gives them dog noses.

"It's weird that you're handing out these flyers all over the school," Stephie says.

"Why? The school elections are for everyone!" retorts Marine, the vice-president, who's following the conversation.

"Because the Gender and Sexuality Alliance elections are mostly a concern for the group's members."

"Well, we think it's the whole school's business. The Alliance needs to remain open to all ideas, even those from students who are against its existence!" says Jérôme-Lou with a brilliant smile.

"Yes, that's a very noble way of thinking," replies my friend through clenched teeth.

I hurry to take her by the arm, and we move away. Once we're gone, I lecture her: "Why did you talk to him? You know he always gets you angry!"

"I wanted to see how far he would go to justify his sense of grandeur."

Imitating Jérôme-Lou's pompous tone, I repeat: *"You already know who's going to win! Ha ha ha."*

Stephie stares at me. "You do that so well, it's scary. Hey, would it bother you if I sat with Zoe in class?"

"Go for it, I'll sit with Liam."

"Ooooh, too cute!"

I shoot her a killer look. She probably won't stop bugging me about Liam until he and I are married with six kids.

When we enter the classroom, we split up as planned and I sit next to Liam, while Stephie greets him before going to sit with her friend in the back of the room.

"So, did you end up falling asleep, finally?" Liam asks me.

We spent last night texting while I was trying to learn about the type of curtain I would need to do my personal project. I was still combing through YouTube when he went to bed.

"Yes, and I slept well! You?"

"Like a brick."

Mrs. Walter, our French teacher, starts handing out the compositions we handed in last class. We had to show that we had understood how to follow a narrative outline, which I found really difficult. I can't seem to focus for very long on a specific subject, and I end up writing whatever I feel like, forgetting that I'm supposed to follow the outline. My dad says that wouldn't stop me from writing a novel, but I don't think Mrs. Walter would agree.

I get my assignment. I can't believe my eyes: I got a B! I kick my feet against my chair with joy and show my mark to Liam. I explain, "The points I lost are in the places where I didn't follow the outline, of course. How did you do?"

He shows me his paper, making a sad face. He got a C. His paper is covered in red ink.

"The teacher wrote that I respected my narrative outline very well, but I have to be careful about errors. That'll teach me to write twice as many words as she asks for!"

"Oh, I'm worse than you for mistakes! If Stephie hadn't helped me correct my composition before handing it in, I would surely have failed."

"Isn't that cheating?" Liam asks, wide-eyed.

"I don't think so…. When you're writing in real life, outside school, you're allowed to ask someone to read it over. I don't plan to become a grammarian or a proofreader, so it's okay. Even with writers who publish books, some of them make tons of errors, but there are people whose job it is to correct them."

"That makes sense, when you put it that way."

"You surely wouldn't want all those people who edit texts to be out of a job, right?"

Liam cracks up. "You're right, it would be a tragedy if everyone knew how to write well!"

"According to my dad, you can succeed at anything if you know how to use your resources. And my main resource is Stephie. You'll have to make friends with her before the next exam!"

"As long as it doesn't involve going to see experimental ballet!"

"Ha ha! We wouldn't have stayed friends long if that's how it worked!"

Mrs. Walter, who has finished giving back our compositions, starts speaking, so we quiet down. But I'd like to talk with Liam for the whole class. I feel so good with him. We could pretend we need to go to the bathroom at the same time so we can keep chatting! But that would surely look suspicious. People might start to get ideas....

I feel myself blushing. I don't even dare look in Liam's direction, I'm afraid it'll get worse. But I'm not imagining anything in particular. Just Liam and me, in a corner of the school, talking...and then kissing, maybe?

Oh my goodness, what if Stephie was right? That Liam and I could be a couple? She's always right, I should know that by now.

Mrs. Walter talks, talks, talks, and I can't catch half of what she's saying. I would definitely have bad grades if Stephie wasn't helping me! The class ends, and I'm still blown away by my epiphany. I'm distracted as I gather up my books.

While we're leaving class, Liam asks, "It's tonight, right? The meeting at the Montréal LGBT+ Center?"

"Uh…yeah. Actually, it's the youth section drop-in."

"Ah, okay. Listen, I forgot to mention it, but I have swim training later."

I try to mask my disappointment. "I understand. Next time, maybe."

"I'm still coming!" he hurries to explain. "The pool is two stations away from Beaudry metro, so I can meet you after."

I feel a little bubble of hope rise in my stomach. "Really? Don't feel obliged to come, of course!"

"Ha ha! It almost sounds like you don't want me to come with you anymore. I was just telling you so you wouldn't be surprised to see me show up with wet hair. My training finishes at five-fifteen, is that okay? I've never gone there before."

"Yes, yes! It's open from five to nine, but we never start the circle discussion until six o'clock. Oh, and there will be food."

"Cool!"

"You want to meet at the metro?"

"Yes, perfect!"

After saying good-bye to Liam, I swing by my locker to get my lunch box, then go find Stephie at our usual table with our little group of friends. Well, they're mostly Stephie's friends, but they're pretty nice and they seem to see me as one of them. I finally ended up learning their names! There's Felicia and Annabelle, who went to the same elementary school as me and Stephie, and then Samira and Zoe, who come to the Gender and Sexuality Alliance meetings with us. As for Liam, if he didn't always go home for lunch, I'd invite him to eat at our table.

When she sees me coming, Zoe cries out, "Silence, everyone! Ciel is here!"

I give her a perplexed look as I sit down next to Stephie. Zoe smiles at me. "You remember, the other day, when we were at the Gender and Sexuality Alliance meeting? We had started to ship you and Stephie because you make the perfect duo."

"Oh yeah! Too true!" says Annabelle.

A little worried, I ask, "Okay, so what?"

"So, I created a graphic representation of this ship, which I've named Stephel. Check it out!"

Zoe pulls a drawing out of her binder and shows it around. It shows a character inspired half by me, half by Stephie. Zoe isn't a great artist, but we can easily see the features that belong to each of us. The other girls exclaim:

"That's Ciel's new haircut!"

"And Stephie's short little nose!"

"Ciel's ripped jeans!"

"The ballet flats Stephie's had since she was ten years old!"

The final touch, the lip gloss that Stephie and I both wear outside school, is the only thing that's not drawn in pencil. Zoe seems to have used a pink gel pen, and the ink shines when you move the paper.

After Stephie and I have taken a few selfies with the Stephel drawing (which she posts right away to Snapchat), Zoe declares, "There you go! Now, you have no choice but to run for leadership of the Gender and Sexuality Alliance!"

Everyone at the table agrees with enthusiasm. I laugh at the suggestion, because there's no question in my mind that it's a joke, but then I notice that Stephie seems uncomfortable. I think I can guess why. I don't hide that I'm trans, to the point where I talk about it on YouTube. But unlike me, my friend does everything she can to make sure as few people as possible know. Only I know, and our friends from elementary school, like Felicia and Annabelle, and Stephie asked us to keep it a secret. When it comes to her presence at the Alliance meetings, she passes as an ally, but she doesn't really want to put a lot of focus on her presence at the group.

She's not ashamed of being trans, but since we started high school, it's reassuring for her to finally be perceived as being just like any other girl, and not always being put in a group apart. I totally understand her, but I don't think it would be possible for me to look like "just any other girl." Among other things because I don't feel entirely like a girl.

Also, I think that if she were openly trans at our school, Stephie wouldn't hesitate for a second to run in the election; she loves that kind of thing. She was a class representative for three years in a row in elementary school. It must be hard for her to explain why she doesn't want to run. To pull her out of the uncomfortable situation, I raise my voice, take the drawing in hand, and say solemnly: "As co-spokesperson of the Stephel coalition, I'd like to humbly thank our fans. It is with great pride that we will hang this work in our offices in the first-year locker wing. However, we cannot run this year, as we want to devote our time to our families. Thank you for understanding. We will not be taking any questions."

"You just need a necktie!" Zoe laughs.

"Yeah, you totally seem like a real politician!" adds Felicia.

"Thank you, thank you."

"I just hope that Jérôme-Lou won't win. That would be terrible," says Samira, pensive, before taking a bite out of her sandwich.

"Who's Jérôme-Lou?" asks Annabelle.

"The current president of the Alliance."

"Oh yeah! The one who keeps shaking everyone's hands?"

"And who says 'ha ha ha' all the time, even when nothing is funny?" adds Felicia.

Stephie, who has regained her composure, joins the conversation. "Yes, but wait, you have to try to understand, even if it's hard. See, Jérôme-Lou is a bit like experimental ballet: he's at a whole other level that's just not accessible to us mere mortals!"

Samira, Zoe, and I start laughing uproariously, while the others smile in silence, not getting the joke.

When we finish eating, we start talking about our schoolwork. We all complain about having too much. Zoe, who also has Mr. Brazeau as a teacher, comments, "For my personal project, I'm going to produce electricity using a lemon. I haven't told Mr. Brazeau, but it's an experiment we did at my summer camp. It's super easy."

"Cool! Me, I'm going to create special effects on my YouTube videos by changing the background."

"Oh! I saw that in a documentary on TV!" says Samira, interested. "In movies, people use a sort of lime green curtain, which they cut out on the computer later to replace it with whatever they want, like another planet, or the belly of a whale."

"Yeah, that's what I've learned so far."

Stephie is doubtful. "And where are you going to put this curtain?"

"Well, in my room. It's not a problem."

She nearly chokes. "In your room?! Your walls are painted caramel, darling. It would be an insult to good taste to hang a lime green curtain!"

"I'll take it down when you come over, don't worry! And anyway, I still don't know where I can find a curtain like that in Montréal."

"Look on Amazon," suggests Annabelle.

"Or at Plaza St-Hubert. There are lots of fabric stores. That's where my mom bought the fabric she used to make my elementary school ball gown," adds Zoe.

"Oh yeah?"

"Yeah! It's near Jean-Talon station."

Stephie turns toward me. "I've got nothing planned for Friday after school! Want to go together?"

"For sure!"

4

The Fantastic Properties of Water

I try to focus on the comic book I borrowed from Virgil in order to impress Liam, but it's hard, especially with all the people coming and going from the metro. I'm sitting on the window sill inside the iconic Beaudry station entrance, which has rainbow columns. From here, I can watch all the people go by. There's no chance I'll miss my friend.

Some fairly young people with dyed hair walk by me. A number of them seem to be heading toward the LGBT+ Center. I bet I'll end up seeing them there soon.

This is the first time Liam and I are really going somewhere together since we've known each other. We've gone shopping or wandered around Chinatown, but nothing structured like today. We're going to meet people, and those people will see us together! They might think we're a couple, even if we're not holding hands or anything.

My heart starts to beat faster at the idea of holding hands. How has this not occurred to me before?

I get a text from Liam.

> *I just got out of the pool, I'm heading to the metro. Be there in 4-5 minutes!*

> *OK!* 😊

I decide to plan what I'll say to him when he gets here. For example, I could ask him, "You didn't get too jostled along the way, I hope? People are terrible at rush hour."

Nah, that might not be the best idea. What if his trip was fine? That would just be embarrassing.

"Well, at least it's not raining!"

No, no, not the weather. That sounds like something a grown-up would say. Who cares if it's not raining!

"Liam! I've missed you so much!"

Hmm, that might be a little much for him. We did just see each other this morning. I wouldn't want him to think I was codependent. I should find a more neutral thing to say.

"Hey! How did your training go?"

Yeah, not sure about that one. He trains, like, thirty-two times a week. I'd be surprised if he wanted to talk about it.

I see his head emerge from the staircase. I get up too quickly and drop the comic book I was trying to read. I bend over awkwardly to pick it up, while Liam makes his way toward me. When I stand up, all I manage to say is, "Ah, hey, your hair is really wet!"

"Told you so. The pool water has a strange tendency to wet things that dive into it."

I laugh a little, feeling ridiculous. Liam adds, "Have you been waiting for me long?"

"No, no, maybe half an hour…."

"Half an hour!"

"Yeah, I knew you said you were finishing at five-fifteen, but I had nothing to do, so I came earlier."

"Oh, okay!"

Without further ado, we start walking toward the LGBT+ Center. I mentally review the scene that just unfolded. "Your hair is really wet!" Seriously? That's the most pathetic thing I could have said. Nothing to be proud of there, Ciel Sousa. He must be laughing at me on the inside. And for good reason. "Your hair is really wet!"

The silence between us thickens. In general, silence doesn't bother me, but right now, it's torture.

I babble, "So, you trained?"

"Yeah, as usual."

What a nightmare. What's wrong with me? I sure hope he trained, it's not called "training" for nothing!

Liam and I have talked almost every day since we met. Why is it that now I can't seem to behave more normally?

We finally arrive at the LGBT+ Center. The room where the youth section meetings take place is located in the basement. It's a big, friendly room with several sofas, computers, a ping-pong table, and a bar in the corner that serves soft drinks, coffee, and hot chocolate. The walls are plastered with posters from tolerance campaigns. A lot of people are already there, including a few of the ones I saw walking by from the metro. I notice that the proportion of kids with natural-colored hair is very low.

We head for the buffet table. A little card shows the name of the neighborhood restaurant that donated the food. It looks pretty tasty: fajitas, burritos, several salads, and veggies and dips. I take two fajitas while Liam fills his plate with everything he can fit on it, under the benevolent eye of the person in charge, a stocky man with a beard whom I remember seeing on my last visit in the spring. He greets us in passing. I look at the badges on his vest, which read "Armand" and "male pronouns" to indicate how to address him. That's relevant in a place like this, where many trans people haven't transitioned yet, or simply can't, for various reasons. There are also young people who dress in atypical ways, like girls in jackets and ties, or boys with crop tops and low-rise jeans, or others, like Mael-a and me, who consider ourselves neither girls nor boys. You can't guess someone's gender just by looking at them.

Liam holds tightly onto his plate, where a mountain of food is piling up in a precarious balance. He exclaims, "I'm so hungry, I could eat everything on the table!"

"I believe you, no need to prove it!"

"Ha ha! Well, where do you want to sit?"

I quickly scan the room: a number of people are eating standing up, others are sitting on the sofas or hanging out in the hallway that leads to the staircase. I notice an empty sofa; it's in the corner where most of the kids are gathered, but it's also the noisiest area, and that's not counting the bright neon lights that are hurting my eyes. I'd rather head for the hallway, where it's quieter, but I'm afraid Liam will think I'm a killjoy.

"The sofa!"

Once we're seated and have started to eat, Liam asks, "Do you know anyone here?"

"At a glance, no. I imagine Mael-a must be here somewhere, since they volunteer here...."

"Oh yeah! That's right. Anyway, I get the feeling we're the youngest."

"Looks that way."

The meal is okay. A little dry for my taste, but it's all right. The noise is unbearable. Liam notices, and suggests, "We could go outside, it's not too cold!"

I agree right away. We pick our way between the people crowded in the hallway. I spot Mael-a, who seems happy to see us. We exchange a few words about my most recent video (they adore Dolores von Tragic and hope she'll make another appearance soon) before announcing that we're going to finish our meal outside.

"See you soon!" Mael-a answers.

The setting sun manages to keep us warm. The inner courtyard of the LGBT+ Center isn't very big. A tree casts its shadow over half the grassy area, which means everyone's squeezed into the same sunny space. We find an open patch of grass and sit down to eat.

Two girls with plates in their hands approach. "Can we sit here?"

"Sure, sure!"

Liam and I move our bags to make room.

"I'm Clementine. This is Sabrina."

"Hi!"

They both look a little older than us, but not by as much as the rest of the people here, so it's less intimidating. Clementine has hair dyed lilac, which contrasts with her neon yellow overalls. Sabrina, her partner, is much taller and is wearing a little black dress over tight jeans. She has mid-length curly brown hair that the wind blows into her mouth. She seems very shy, much more so than I am. Maybe this is the first time she's wearing a dress in public? That wouldn't surprise me, as she keeps adjusting it and smoothing the wrinkles out.

We introduce ourselves in turn. Clementine asks, "Do you often come to the drop-in?"

"No," says Liam. "You?"

"I've come a few times, myself, but this is only Sabrina's second time. We were here two weeks ago."

"Yeah. We come in from Bois-des-Filion, on the North Shore. To get here, it takes an hour and a half by bus and metro."

"Whoa!"

"There's another youth group in Saint-Jérôme, but it takes even longer to get there because of the buses," adds Clementine.

"And I was the only trans person there," says Sabrina. "We were the youngest ones, too, so it was a little uncomfortable."

Liam and I exchange a smile. I comment, "Yeah, we know what that's like, being the youngest ones."

"Oh, stop! You're what, fourteen?"

"Twelve."

"We're both fifteen."

"It's still unbelievable that you have to come such a long way to attend this kind of meeting," says Liam.

Clementine and Sabrina both shrug, resigned. Without thinking, I say, "I could make a video about this on my YouTube channel. Explain that there aren't enough resources for LGBT youth."

"You have a YouTube channel?" asks Clementine, interested.

"Yeah! Well, it's no big deal, I'm not that good."

Liam protests, "That's not true! You're very good. Your videos always get me thinking, whether they're funny or more serious. They're never boring!"

I can't help blushing. "Thanks, that's nice."

"Okay, I have to see this," says Sabrina. "What's your channel called? I'll subscribe!"

"Me too!"

They both take out their phones. Sabrina exclaims, when she sees the list of videos, "Too cool! You've got so many! Do you make them all yourself?"

"Yeah, with my brother. My friend Stephie helps sometimes, too."

"I'd love to create a YouTube channel, but my videos always look way amateur."

"The important thing is to edit the video properly. That can take some time."

While we've been talking, the kids who were indoors have gradually come out to join the gathering in the courtyard.

Once everyone's sitting in a big circle, Armand and Mael-a give a little introduction, talk a bit about the LGBT+ Center and the services they provide for us, and then introduce the talking hat for us to pass around. When we receive it, we have to say our name, the pronouns we use, and—if we want—what we want to do later in life or if we have dreams for the future.

I want to say that my name is Ciel, without saying anything more. It stresses me out to see my turn coming, to the point where I can't focus on what other people are saying. It's like this every time, I hate speaking in front of a group.

Finally, the talking hat lands in my hands. I quietly say my name and pronouns before handing the hat over to Liam, as if it had burned my fingers. I don't even hear what he says, or anyone after him. My heartbeat is barely getting back to its usual rhythm.

Once everyone has spoken, Mael-a asks whether anyone has news to share with the group. Hands go up. Two people went to see the Lady Gaga show last weekend. One boy shyly announces that he found a boyfriend at school. Everyone feels sweet about it. Even I join in with a tender "aww!"

We continue this way for a few minutes, and the discussion ends. It's pretty short, and I enjoy it: here, the focus is on sharing a space and meeting each other, unlike the Alliance meetings, where we usually talk about rules, events to plan, and funding. Armand reminds us about the date of the next meeting, in two weeks, and tells us he's available until nine o'clock if anyone wants to speak with him privately in his office.

While a few people head inside or leave, our little group remains seated on the grass so we can talk. The sun is down, now, and it's starting to get chilly. Sabrina suggests, "Do you want to go get a hot chocolate? There's a café just across from the metro."

I look at Liam, who stammers, "Uh…I don't really have the money…."

"Oh, but Clementine is treating!" says Sabrina, smiling at her girlfriend.

We turn toward Clementine, who agrees. Sabrina leans over to Liam and me and adds, "I was uncomfortable letting her pay for things at first, but her family has lots of money. It's a way of redistributing wealth."

Liam smiles. "Okay, in that case, let's go."

We leave by a little door in the fence surrounding the LGBT+ Center courtyard. The trees, chilled by the rain from the last few days, are dropping leaves at the faintest hint of a breeze.

When we enter the café Sabrina had mentioned, our nostrils are filled with a strong sweet smell. The place is pretty packed, but we manage to find a big enough table for all four of us near the back. Clementine takes our orders: a caramel frappé for me, a strawberry one for Sabrina, and a hot chocolate for Liam. She waits in line while we chat.

I feel strangely sophisticated sitting with friends at a café. It's not something I normally do. I don't mention it, because I'm afraid of seeming like a baby to my new, older friends. I'll have to ask Stephie if she'd like to do this with me. She and her mom often go read in this kind of place. Sometimes, I imagine it's the sort of thing I would have done with my own mother.

Clementine comes back with our drinks, while Liam's phone starts ringing. He answers. "Hi, Mom! Yes…yes, very. We're in a café, we're…. What? Yeah, yeah, don't worry. See you later!"

"That was fast," says Sabrina once Liam hangs up.

"Yeah. That was my mom. She doesn't like me staying out too late."

Clementine sighs. "It's nice that she called you. Since I told my parents I'm a lesbian last month, it's as if I've suddenly become a stranger. They barely talk to me.

They say they need time to get used to it."

Sabrina takes her hand, to comfort her, and says, "I'm luckier than she is. I have two lesbian moms, and they're always super understanding. They supported me when I transitioned last year."

"How have your parents taken it?" asks Clementine.

I look at Liam to see if he wants to answer first. He says, "My mom, pretty well. Sometimes she says the wrong thing, but she does her best. My dad, though.... It's a good thing I don't see him often! He's the type to send me cards that say 'to my beloved daughter' with a ballerina and glitter. We've never been very close, so it doesn't bother me much. He lives in Gaspésie."

Clementine and Sabrina nod, then look at me.

"My dad has always let me dress how I want at home, so when I asked him to use another name and pronouns, it didn't surprise him too much."

"And your mom?" asks Clementine.

"She died a few years ago."

A heavy silence descends on the group.

Clementine looks shocked. "I'm...I'm sorry."

"It's okay, don't worry about it." I feel guilty for killing the mood, and I hurry to change the subject. "Do any of you know the musical *Lafontaine*? My best friend Stephie and I are going to see it in November. I got tickets for my birthday!"

Liam starts laughing. "Here we go, when Ciel starts talking about *Lafontaine*, it's impossible to stop them."

"Not only do we know it, but we went to see it last week!" says Clementine. "Sabrina's mom got VIP tickets from her job!"

"Lucky you!"

We talk about the show long enough to bore Liam, and then Sabrina says, "Well, Clementine and I have to go. This was really fun, though!"

I suggest, "We should take a selfie!"

After a dozen tries, Clementine succeeds in taking a shot where everyone's eyes are open. She promises to send it to us. We put our jackets on as we exchange Instagram and Snapchat profiles.

Before we head out the door, Sabrina asks, "Do you mind if I go to the bathroom first?"

"Not at all, go ahead!"

Sabrina heads to the cash to ask the employee for the key. He holds out a big wooden spatula with a key attached to the bottom. Sabrina makes her way down the hall toward the bathroom. She comes out right away, though, visibly annoyed. She goes back to the employee and says, "You gave me the wrong key. This is for the men's bathroom."

"Yeah."

"Could I get the women's?"

The employee looks her up and down, and says, "I don't think so, no."

I let out a little shocked cry. I can't believe my ears! How dare he say that? I look at Liam, who has gone pale, and Clementine, who seems enraged.

Sabrina turns a deep red. Without a word, she throws the wooden spatula down on the counter and comes back to us with her teeth gritted, completely thrown off. She makes a huge effort to hold back her tears.

Clementine takes her hand and asks, "Do you want me to go talk to him?"

"What, you're going to tell him he's an imbecile?"

"No, I'll punch him in the face."

Sabrina shakes her head and pulls Clementine outside. We follow them, giving the employee angry looks.

There are better ways to end an evening.

5

Stay Slick, Chick

True to my habit, I wake up two minutes before my alarm rings. I unglue Virgil from my arm, which he's drooled all over. When I got in last night, I found him dozed off in my bed. That happens more rarely now that we don't share a room. I admit I miss it a bit, even if he can be gross when he's asleep, as my wet arm can testify.

Liam and I had taken the metro together. It gave us a chance to decompress after that rude employee ruined an otherwise perfect evening. Liam was sad for Sabrina and was already planning to attend the next drop-in, in case she and Clementine came back. He was afraid the café incident would discourage her from going out. I promised I would keep him in the loop if I decided to go.

Just before my stop, I suddenly started daydreaming, imagining that he was kissing me on the metro seat. It didn't happen. Maybe that's for the best. I'd like my first kiss with Liam to last, not be cut short by the STM bell warning us that the door is closing.

Instead of taking the bus, I walked through Parc Maisonneuve to get home. I had hoped to catch a glimpse of one of the foxes that live there, it would have been a good omen. I didn't see any, but instead, in the wide-open sky, I was able to clearly see the constellations—the Big Dipper and Cassiopeia. My mother taught me to recognize them, so I decided that would be my good omen. I stretched out on the grass for a few minutes to look at them, and I took the opportunity to answer my dad's text to let him know everything was fine and I'd be home soon. I should have done that when I was leaving the café, but with everything that happened, I completely forgot.

I'd also texted Stephie to tell her about my night. She wasn't finished babysitting and tried to convince me to come over. No such luck; I was very much looking forward to being in my bed. I couldn't help telling her about my crush on Liam. She was too proud of herself. "I knew it! I totally saw it coming. You're perfect together!" I'm a little nervous about seeing her at school in a bit.... I hope she won't spill the beans in front of Liam.

I finally get out of bed, after checking out Facebook, Instagram, and Snapchat to see what's going on. I took the opportunity to look through Clementine and Sabrina's profiles. I really thought they were nice. I don't know if I can call them my friends yet, it might be too soon.

I've barely taken two steps out of my room before Borki shows up and starts rubbing against my legs.

"Good dog! Hey, go wake up Virgil!"

Borki jumps up on my bed, goes looking for my little brother's face, and sticks his cold nose on it. Virgil doesn't even notice; he automatically reaches out to snuggle the dog while staying fast asleep. Borki curls up next to him and whines. I sigh and leave.

My dad is in the kitchen, making our lunches. I say hi while I make a bowl of cereal. He says hello and asks if Virgil is up yet.

"No, and he doesn't seem anywhere near awake."

"Oh, that kid! Did you sleep well?"

"Not bad."

"So how did your meeting go? Did you and Liam have fun?"

"Lots! We met two girls from outside Montréal, who had to travel for nearly two hours to be there!"

Because I want him to let me keep going, I avoid telling him about how the evening ended. Instead, I continue, "The parents of one girl are rich, so she treated us to a café after the event."

"That's very nice of her! What's her name?"

"Clementine. And she has a trans girlfriend, Sabrina."

"Wow! I'm surprised you were so sociable. That's a new thing!"

I stop eating my cereal for a moment. It's true that I'm not in the habit of making friends so easily. I'm more the type to stick with people I know, and I need really good reasons to force myself to come out of my bubble. I wonder if it's because I've changed in the last few weeks...or if, subconsciously, I was trying to impress Liam.

"Yeah, I'm looking forward to the next drop-in."

My dad smiles nervously. He seems hesitant. After a short silence, he speaks in the careful voice he uses when he knows what he's about to say might upset me. "Uh, I was talking with Myriam yesterday. Would it bother you if she came apple-picking with us at Saint-Joseph-du-Lac this weekend?"

The news doesn't surprise me that much. I've suspected for a while now that things might be getting more serious between my dad and his girlfriend. I like Myriam a lot, and I've gradually gotten used to her presence, and to that of Leah, her sixteen-year-old daughter, who joins us for things once in a while. But this time, it's different: apple-picking is an annual tradition we had with my mother. As well, legend has it that my parents went together for their first date, after they met at university during a summer course. My dad had just left Brazil to spend six months in Québec and hadn't yet seen the trees turn red in the fall.

So, it bothers me that Myriam will be coming with us. Still, I think I'm being a bit immature to let myself feel affected by this kind of detail, so I plaster a smile on my face and answer, "No, why would it bother me?"

"I just wanted to get your opinion. Also, if she comes, it'll be easier for us because she has a car!"

"It's true that it's usually complicated…. When we want to get home, we have to take a taxi to the station, then the train to the metro, with our big bags of apples! Actually, it's kind of funny."

"Funny? You're not the one who has to schlep most of the bags!"

We laugh for a moment, then I decide to use my dad's sense of guilt to get a favor out of him.

"Oh! You know my personal project for my science and technology class? Stephie and I are going shopping tomorrow after school to try to find a curtain, and I was wondering…."

"How much do you need?" my dad interrupts quickly.

"I don't know yet. I don't think it'll cost me more than thirty or forty dollars."

My dad goes to get his wallet and takes out two twenties. "Bring me back the change."

"Thanks, Dad!"

I hug him from my chair before letting him get back to the counter to finish making lunch.

♥ ♥ ♥

Stephie isn't at school yet when I get to our locker, which has changed a lot since our first day. At first, it was less messy, obviously, but it also had a little mirror I had bought at the pharmacy. Unfortunately, it fell and broke once when I slammed the door too hard because I was running late to class. To replace it, Stephie added a wall-mounted notepad that came with a pen, and we leave each other messages or drawings from time to time. For a few days now, it has displayed a drawing of a chicken Stephie made, and underneath she wrote, "Stay slick, chick." I tear off the sheet so I can glue it in my agenda later.

I take the pen off its magnet and start drawing a fish that says, "Peace out, trout." The result is funny, but not as pretty as Stephie's drawing. Pff! She's already the smarter one in our duo, couldn't she let me be the artist?

Speaking of duos, we still have the Stephel portrait that Zoe drew. We stuck it on the locker door right under the notepad. Even though it's not perfect, I think it's super cute. Stephie and I better not have a fight, we'd never be able to decide who would get to keep it!

Stephie arrives and gives me a little hug.

"How's my Juliet doing?"

"Huh? Juliet?"

"Yes, like in *Romeo and Juliet*. Liam is your Romeo."

"Hmm. I'd rather not, no. Could I be Romeo instead? But like, a feminine version of Romeo... Romeliet?"

"Romeliet and Julio?"

"Oh yes, that's much better."

"If you insist!"

"Yes, Romeliet works for me. Can you still come shopping with me tomorrow? My dad gave me money for my curtain!"

"It's on my calendar!"

She opens her agenda and shows me her Friday column. At the bottom, in the last box, she had written in pink: "Operation find a lime green curtain/an insult to good taste for Ciel's room."

Stephie sees my amused look and explains, "I didn't

have enough room to add other synonyms. I thought about 'a torture device for the eyes,' 'a soul-killer in textile form,' 'a chromatic cataclysm....'"

I laugh. Stephie loves to lay it on thick. While she finishes getting ready for class, I ask, "Did your babysitting go well last night?"

"Yes and no. Momo's parents came home nearly two hours late, but they gave me double my pay."

"Wow!"

"Apart from that, I spent the night reading and watching TV on their curved-screen while stuffing my face with popcorn...all alone again!"

"Poor little thing. Do you need a hug?" I take her in my arms as she pretends to cry. I pat her back. "Hush, hush. Think of everything you'll be able to buy at Plaza St-Hubert."

Right away, she's back on her feet and smiling.

"You're absolutely right! Pink Flamingo is in the neighborhood. It's my favorite store for clothing and accessories. Could we go there tomorrow?"

"Only after we've found my 'chromatic cataclysm!'"

♥ ♥ ♥

At lunch, I sit with Stephie and the others at our usual table. Felicia starts telling an interminable story about her dad, who builds collectible cars. Bored of the subject, I sneak my phone out of my pocket and I notice that YouTube is showing tons of notifications: fifty new people have subscribed to my channel! It's been a long time since I saw that kind of jump. I read the new comments, mostly on my most recent video about inclusion policies at school. Clearly, my brother's appearance as Dolores von Tragic is a real hit. Other people have watched my most popular videos, like the one about the bathrooms at my high school. I wonder where this sudden attention is coming from.

All of a sudden, I hear people cheering. I lift my head. A blonde boy wearing a baseball cap stands up on a bench as the students around him encourage him. I notice that he's holding one of the flyers Jérôme-Lou was handing out the other day. He starts to make a non-sense speech.

"Hello, hello everyone! I'm Geoffrey Levasseur, third-year student, and I'll be running in the school elections for the LGBCDEFG-whatever Alliance. Vote for me, and I'll add ninety-nine new gender options on your student cards. In addition to being able to identify as a 'girl' or a 'boy,' you'll now be able to choose 'dragon,' 'mayonnaise,' and 'attack helicopter.' As well, under my rule, the school will allow girls to go pee in the boys' bathrooms, and guys to go pee in the girls' bathrooms. Vote for Geoffrey!"

Some students applaud and others boo while he gets down off the bench. He rejoins his group of friends, laughing and giving them high-fives. Slumped in my chair, I'm so discouraged I don't have the strength to be angry. Samira, however, raises her voice so that everyone at the nearby tables can hear her.

"Come on, are you kidding? Why is he allowed to say stupid stuff like that, in front of the whole school, no less? Boo!"

She quiets down quickly when she sees Jérôme-Lou's gelled hair making its way toward the bench where Geoffrey had stood. He stands up and exclaims: "Ha ha ha. Such a joker, that Geoffrey! Welcome to the race."

The boy's voice calls out, "I was kidding, you big fag."

Jérôme-Lou waves his hands and laughs, ignoring the comment. "Jokes or no, as the current president of the Gender and Sexuality Alliance, I think dialogue is the most important part of opening people's hearts, and that we need to listen to the various opinions of our wonderful community at Simonne Monet-Chartrand."

I choke with rage. How dare he congratulate Geoffrey for his horrible speech?

All of a sudden, Samira leaps up. She yells at Jérôme-Lou, "That was an insult to trans people! We can't just let it go!"

Jérôme-Lou seems shocked for a moment, but he quickly finds his smile again. "Excuse me, but we won't make any progress with hate. In my view, we need love! Ha ha ha. That's why I want to take this opportunity to unveil my election campaign slogan: 'Love wins!' Vote for Jérôme-Lou!"

I look at Stephie, who seems completely over-whelmed. We can't believe our ears. It comes as no surprise that a third-year idiot would say ridiculous things like what we just heard. But for the president of the Gender and Sexuality Alliance, who's supposed to represent us and defend us, to approve of them and even encourage them? That's profoundly messed up.

Samira sits down in a fury. She takes a deep breath and turns toward us. "No, I've had enough. If nobody wants to run against Jérôme-Lou, I will. I'm not afraid of him."

She pauses and looks around the people at the table. "However, I'm going to need someone to be my running mate. Anyone ready to volunteer?"

The other girls exchange questioning glances. Apparently, nobody else is interested, not even Zoe. Stephie reddens and bites her lip. I see in her face that it's torture for her to hold back after a scene like that. She clears her throat and says, in a small voice, "Well, if nobody else—"

I interrupt her. "Me. I'll do it. I'll be your teammate, Samira."

6

Québec's Got Talent

I'm leaning against the locker waiting for Stephie so we can go shopping at Plaza St-Hubert. To pass the time, I'm fooling around on my phone. YouTube tells me I have more new subscribers to my channel, which is kind of unusual. I go check how many times my last video has been viewed, and the number is growing. Wow! Too cool!

I try to focus on the good news to help me forget what happened yesterday in the cafeteria. I'm still in shock. Running in the school elections! *Me!* I still can't get over that I managed to do that. As if strangers would want to vote for me when they stop me in the hallways to ask if I'm a boy or a girl! Honestly, it wouldn't upset me in the least if Samira and I were to lose. I don't want to be the vice-president of the Gender and Sexuality

Alliance, and I certainly don't want to sit on student council. But Samira seems so happy to team up with me that I can't really see myself stepping back.... She must have sent me thirty texts since yesterday (even in the afternoon, during her phys ed class, I have no idea how). We're going to meet up on Sunday to talk about our ideas and start creating our posters, but we still haven't even officially signed up as candidates! To do that, we have to fill out a kind of form at Guy's office, the person in charge of student life. Samira said she'll take care of it Monday.

A familiar voice draws my eyes up off my screen. "Hey, Ciel! How's it going?"

It's Mael-a, who's with a guy, probably someone also in fourth year.

"It's so cool what's happening for you on Twitter!"

"Oh, thanks!"

"Of course! Congrats!" Mael-a gives me a warm smile.

After a silence, I admit, "But, um...I'm not on Twitter. What happened?"

"You didn't know? Lydia Dynamite shared your most recent video on her account!"

"Who's Lydia Dynamite?"

"She's the Montréal drag queen who won on the *Québec's Got Talent* show last year!"

"Ah, yes, I see." I pretend to understand what Mael-a's talking about so I don't look ignorant, but this means nothing to me. I almost never watch that kind of show on TV!

Mael-a pulls their phone out of their shirt pocket and asks their friend to wait for a minute. They open the Twitter app and scroll down their feed to the post in question. "Here, there it is."

The profile pic shows a person wearing exaggerated, caricatured makeup. Lydia Dynamite is wearing an enormous, flamboyant wig and a chic silver dress and has a sparkling smile and a confident expression. She looks really impressive! Above my video, her comment reads, "A very promising little drag queen and a young trans person talk about real life with style! A channel you'll want to follow!"

The post has seven hundred and ninety-eight likes and two hundred and thirty-six retweets. That must be where all the hits on my video have come from, and surely a lot of my new subscribers too! I thank Mael-a, who wishes me a good night and hurries off to join their friend.

I feel very proud. The fact that a star is recommending my channel is an awesome recognition of my work…and Virgil's, of course. When my brother sees what his acting talents have brought to my video, he'll flip! I open Instagram and look for Lydia Dynamite. She's easy to find—her name and her orange wig are pretty unique. On her profile, she's got tons of pictures of herself in hilarious poses. I hit the "follow" button, and just then, Stephie arrives along with Frank.

"Sorry I'm late!" she says.

"What were you doing?"

"Uh…I was wishing Frank good luck for his soccer game tonight."

"For ten minutes?"

Frank shoots back, "I need a lot of luck!"

"Right. Yeah."

Stephie makes puppy dog eyes at me. "Do you mind if Frank comes with us? He's got an hour and a half to kill before the game."

"Not at all, of course. As long as you don't spend all your time smooching, though…."

"We'll just hold hands. I can hold your hand too, so you don't feel jealous," my friend says with a smile.

She takes Frank's hand, and mine, and we leave school to head to the bus stop. I tell them about my new video's success.

Frank exclaims, "Lydia Dynamite noticed your channel?! That's amazing, congratulations!"

I'm stunned. "You know her?"

"Of course! She was the winner of *Québec's Got*

Talent last year. Her song 'Don't Bother Me in the Morning' often plays on the radio, too."

Stephie smiles at him. "You're so knowledgeable about pop culture, my love."

"And you know everything about culture, period."

The two gaze at each other lovingly. I exclaim, "Okay, that's enough with the cow eyes!"

"You should follow our example and teach yourself to make eyes at people, since you'll be running in the school election!" comments Stephie with a mean look.

"Not gonna happen. Plus, I'm not that excited about this election. I just wanted to help Samira."

"I'm sure you'll be an excellent vice-president."

Frank adds, "I agree! It's clear in your videos. You know what you're talking about."

Stephie pats my shoulder. "Also, it's a great opportunity to make friends with Samira. She's super nice."

"Well, she has lots of ideas for our campaign." I scroll through all the messages Samira sent me throughout the day.

Her long blocks of text are followed by my short answers: "Yup!" "Okay." "Good idea! ☺"

"She seems motivated!"

We arrive at Plaza St-Hubert. There are lots of people on the sidewalk, and they all seem in a hurry. A little too in a hurry, even. It feels like they're trying to run into us on purpose! We cross Rue Jean-Talon, which is bottlenecked with rush-hour traffic.

Frank asks, "What are we going to get exactly? Stephie explained that you wanted to redecorate your room with some evil fabric that might open a portal to a parallel dimension filled with demons, but I'm not sure I know what that looks like."

I throw Stephie an exasperated look. She smiles and shrugs.

"It's for my science and tech project."

"You're gonna do black magic?! I can't believe Mr. Brazeau approved! Though I guess it's true he's in a punk band—"

"I am not! I'm creating a backdrop for filming my videos, which I'll then be able to change using the computer."

"Oh." Frank makes a serious face, and adds, "Anyway, you're lucky, Ciel. I still don't have a topic for my personal project. Mr. Brazeau wants me to do it on clocks, unless I have a better idea by Monday."

"Come on, I'm sure you can come up with something better than a project on clocks!"

Frank shrugs, resigned, while Stephie rolls her eyes.

♥ ♥ ♥

Zoe was right: there are tons of fabric stores in the area, so many that it's hard to pick one. The first ones we see look a bit too focused on bridal gowns: there's lace, satin, and tulle in the window, all of it white. We finally spot a boutique that looks a little less fancy.

A bell rings when we enter. A man built like a truck moves in front of us, holding a long, thick roll of fabric on his shoulder. "Hello, my friends! Give me a moment, I'll be right with you."

He heads toward a corner of the store where there's a mountain of rolls in various sizes, colors, and textures, and places the one he was carrying on top. As he does this, I look around: the walls are covered in shelves, like in a library, except that instead of books, they hold fabric rolled around pieces of rectangular cardboard. Near the cash, there's a display case filled with thread, needles, measuring tape, and more. A huge wooden table reigns over the center of the shop, like a control tower in an airport.

"So, what can I do for you?"

I speak up before Stephie can start describing my project in some terrifying way. "Well, I make videos, see, and I'm looking for a kind of curtain that could serve as a background, which I could then edit on my computer to replace it with images."

"I see! Something in a solid, then?"

"Uh…."

"You want it in just one color?"

"Yes. Normally it's neon green. I read that it's easier to digitally alter that."

"You're not the only boy to…the only girl, I mean… or boy?" The salesman gives me a questioning look.

I answer, "Person."

"You're not the first person to ask me that. Someone came just the other day, and I gave him this." The salesman beckons me to follow him to the fabric library. He tugs on a bolt of lime green cloth a bit to show it to me.

"It's a basic cotton, pretty thick, that will absorb the light well."

"Okay," I say, a little disoriented by all the information.

"There's another one I'm thinking of. I think it's in the corner with the rolls over there." He lays the cotton (as he called it) on the big central table, and then we cross the store toward the mountain of rolls. He scans the tubes quickly, then pulls one out. It's a less bright shade of green.

"This one is a synthetic fabric. It's a little less thick than the cotton and won't absorb the light as well, but the advantage is that it doesn't wrinkle as much as the other one: it will stay soft and flat." He scrunches a corner of the fabric to show me. "It's also half as expensive. I can set them side by side if you want to compare."

He pulls the roll out of the pile and brings it to the table. Stephie inspects the fabrics and runs her fingers over them. She looks very knowledgeable, so I imitate her.

"Do you prefer one of the two?" the salesman asks me.

"The cotton. I like its texture."

He sets the roll of synthetic fabric on the floor behind the table. He spreads the cotton very flat in front of him and, picking up a gigantic pair of scissors, he asks, "And how much do you want?"

"Uh…what does two meters look like?"

With an expert movement, he pulls on the corner of the cotton to unroll it on the table. "It looks like all this."

"That should be enough."

Impressed, Frank comments, "You've got an eye! You can tell how much two meters is just like that, by looking?"

The salesman laughs and shows Frank the edge of the table. "There's a ruler embedded here."

Once he's unrolled the right amount of fabric, he cuts a little notch in it with his big pair of scissors. Then he sets down the scissors, grabs the two sides of the notch with his fingers, and rips the cotton from end to end with a loud sound that makes me jump.

"But why are you destroying it?" asks Stephie, shocked.

The salesman smiles and beckons us to come near. "You see how the threads form straight lines in the fabric?"

We lean over the table to look at the cotton.

He continues, "With my scissors, I can't follow those lines, which means the fabric might start to fray. But if I rip it, I have a better chance of going in the same direction as the weave. Look how straight it is!" He points at the piece of cloth.

Frank lets out an admiring "Whoa."

"Where did you learn all this?"

"At school. I was a garment-making student."

Frank's eyes widen as if he's just had a revelation. "You know how to sew?"

"Of course. I made all the clothes I'm wearing, except my socks!"

Suddenly, all our eyes are riveted on him: we scrutinize his vest, his shirt, his pants.

"You're very good!" says Stephie.

"Thanks! I hope to work for a fashion house when I'm finished my studies."

"You want to be a designer?"

"No, just a sewer. I like working with my hands, feeling the fabric between my fingers, seeing the pieces come together. The design part is mostly drawing, pattern-making, research. It's important, but it's not what I like best. Also, everyone wants to be a designer; the competition is fierce."

He scribbles the name of the fabric and how much I took on a scrap of paper, then holds out the paper and the cotton he's carefully folded. He turns toward an open door behind the cash register and calls out something in what sounds like Arabic. A raspy voice responds in the same language, and the salesman says to us, "You can go see my friend at the cash to pay!"

Frank, who's getting quite a few surprises, exclaims, "You speak Arabic?"

"Of course! I'm Lebanese."

"Really? Me too!"

Well, we've lost them. They start speaking Arabic together. Meanwhile, Stephie and I head toward the cash, where a bearded man greets us. Once I've paid and the fabric is safely stowed in my backpack, we return to the cutting table, where Frank and the salesman are deep in an animated discussion. The salesman laughs loudly and says, in English, "Wait for me just a minute, I'll be right back. I have something for you, Frank." He heads toward the back of the shop.

Stephie asks Frank, "What were you talking about?"

"About school, stuff like that. I told him I'd like to learn to sew for my science project, but my mom probably wouldn't let me."

The salesman comes back and holds a packet out to Frank. "Here, my guy, I'm giving you this. It's a beginner pattern, we stopped selling it a while ago. The instructions are in the envelope, it's to make the shorts you see on the picture. And this is a piece of denim big enough to make them with. We can't sell it because it's torn at the bottom, but it will still work."

"You're so nice, sir!" Frank replies, totally wowed.

"Oh, call me Ashraf! Come back and see me, if you want, if you have questions. And good luck with your school project!"

7

Supreme Shopping Advice

As promised, when we leave the fabric store, we head to
Pink Flamingo, the clothing boutique Stephie adores.
Frank, who's barely recovered from his emotions, has to
go back to school for his soccer game, and we say good-
bye on the sidewalk.

The boutique, located two blocks away, is pretty
small. The prices seem exorbitant. I don't even want
to look at anything, because I know I won't be able to
buy it. Stephie, however, always dives in with abandon.
Without being superficial, she likes to feel beautiful,
and even when she knows she won't buy anything, she
enjoys the experience of putting on pretty clothes. It
boosts her spirits. When she fought with her father a
few weeks ago, that's what we did, and it only took two
dresses before her mood improved.

This time, it's different, because she can spend her babysitting money. I have to say, Momo's parents have been particularly generous with her.

When we open the door to the store, Stephie says excitedly, "You need to help me, Ciel. I can't spend everything. Repeat our supreme shopping advice, please."

"You're not obliged to buy anything. Take the time to think about what you want. Ask yourself if you really need the—"

"*OH MY GOD!* Look at that fox print! It's too cute, it's totally you. You have to try it on."

"I'm not finished with the supreme advice! Be courteous with the sales staff, their job can sometimes be hard—"

"Well, *I'm* going to try it on."

She drapes the fox-print jacket over her arm and continues looking at the racks, while I follow her, resigned.

She asks me, "Do you have plans for the weekend?"

"Tomorrow, we're going apple-picking in Saint-Joseph-du-Lac."

"Ooooh! That means your dad will be baking pie. You'll have to invite me over!"

"I have no plans for after that. Want to come sleep over?"

"That would be fun. Frank wants to go to the movies, but we can go Sunday."

"Yeah. On Sunday, I have to help Samira with the poster campaign for the election."

"Oh yes, that's right!"

She's now got five pieces over her arm; apart from the jacket, she found four dresses covered in buttons and ribbons.

A saleswoman approaches us. "I can put those aside for you, if you want to keep looking."

"No, thanks, I'll try them right away."

We follow the saleswoman to the fitting rooms. She hangs the clothes on a hook and lets Stephie in; Stephie draws the curtain closed behind her. Sitting on a little bench to the side, I hear Stephie crashing around as she tries to put on her overly complicated dresses. I can't help getting lost in my thoughts. After a moment, I say out loud, "I'm not sure I feel like going tomorrow. Myriam, my dad's special friend, is coming with us."

"You don't like her?"

"No, it's not that. She's very nice. It's just that apple-picking is something we did every year with my mom."

"And you get the sense she's taking your mother's place."

"Hmm. When you say it like that, no. I know she'll never take her place."

Stephie pulls back the curtain and spins in her flowered yellow dress. "Yes, but that's still what you're feeling. There's no shame in feeling that way. When my parents separated, I was angry at every new person my dad or my mom met, even if they were the best in the world. What do you think?"

"I think that's stupid of me. It wouldn't have bothered me for Myriam to come with us if she and my dad hadn't gotten so serious. And also, she has a car."

"No! What do you think of the dress?"

"Ah. It's pretty! Both chic and casual. You could wear it to school, but you could also wear it to important events. The color suits you. Show me the other ones!"

Stephie goes back into the fitting room. She says, "So, when do you plan to tell Liam you like him?"

"Uh, I don't know. I don't even know if I want to do that. I'm not in a hurry. Things are working well as they are. I don't want to spoil everything by moving too quickly."

"Liam is cool. You're his only friend at school. You won't spoil anything."

She opens the curtain again. This time, she's wearing a long black dress with a lace collar. "Does it scare you?"

"Well, you look like you're coming from a funeral. With the right makeup, you could maybe look like a zombie, but I wouldn't go so far as to say it really *scares* me."

"Huh? I'm talking about you telling Liam you like him!"

"Oops! Sorry."

She closes the curtain again, letting out a deep sigh.

My friend finally decides on a pale pink dress with a crocheted top, which looks very tame, and a pair of socks with a print of cats in astronaut costumes (she couldn't resist). She checks her phone as we leave the store.

"My dad's expecting me for dinner. Do you want me to come over after to help you install the curtain?"

"Sure, sounds good!"

♥ ♥ ♥

When I step into the apartment, no surprise, I find Virgil on the computer. I pull him away from his game to tell him that Lydia Dynamite shared my video on Twitter, and that her comment said he was a promising drag queen.

"Too cool! But uh…who's Lydia Dynamite?"

I explain it to him. He gets very excited and exclaims, "Well in that case, we'll have to make sure Dolores von Tragic makes another appearance!"

"Speaking of that, I'll need your permission to post this little video as a bonus." I take out my phone and play the few seconds I filmed this week, in which we see Dolores von Tragic eating dinner and spilling a piece of hot broccoli down her dress; she can't get it out and lets out a "*merda!*" with great feeling.

"Ha ha ha! Yeah, go for it, you can put that online. João will find it so funny!"

I admire Virgil's ability to not take himself seriously. The video is hilarious, but I wouldn't have wanted it to end up on the Internet if I was the one in it. That's why I made sure to get his approval before posting it.

I go say hi to my dad, who's busy making dinner. He looks up from the mixing bowl and asks me, "So, did you find what you wanted for your project?"

"I think so. I hope it does the trick. It's a cotton fabric. The salesman told me it would absorb the light well."

"Got it! Let me know how it goes."

"Is it okay if Stephie comes by later to help me hang it in my room?"

"Of course. How did you plan to hang the fabric on the wall?"

"I don't really know. Maybe with some knots or some rope...."

"You can use the hammer that's in the tool cupboard. There should be a box of nails next to it."

"Okay, I'll take a look."

I disappear into my room to edit the Virgil video. I'm proud of the title I come up with: *The Great Comeback of Dolores von Tragic*. It will surprise people. I post it online, but I don't have time to see my subscribers' reactions because dinner is ready. Our family rule is that we don't bring our phones to the table.

After dinner, I hang out in the living room to wait for Stephie. She sent me a text saying she'd be getting here soon. Virgil's getting ready to go out with Borki. I stop him as he goes by and show him the comments the video has gotten so far:

"Hahahahaha!"

"*Merda!*"

"You're my idol, Dolores von Tragic!"

"Broccoli is so dangerous."

"Hahaha!" (Again.)

"OMG!"

In short, it's a success across the board! As he leaves, Virgil is gamboling with so much energy that Borki gets excited and starts barking at the end of his leash.

Shortly after that, Stephie arrives. "I passed your brother as I came in. He was so happy to tell me he was going to be a star."

"Talk about a big head!"

"Stop, he's too adorable!"

"Being adorable and having an inflated ego—it's not necessarily a contradiction! I put the broccoli video online earlier."

"Ah, yes, the one you showed me the other day? That kid is destined for greatness."

Without further ado, we go to my room. I've spread the cotton fabric on the bed to inspect it.

"So I was thinking of hanging it in this corner, against the wall facing the window, to get the most natural light possible."

Stephie grimaces. "Are you sure? It's going to be really ugly!"

"Give it up! I don't care that it's going to be ugly."

"It's just that I don't want you calling me at midnight saying you've had nightmares and you want me to come help you take it down!"

"Come on, no. I'm going to nail it to the wall. It will be easy to take down, I'll just have to pull on it."

Stephie sighs in disapproval. Still, we go get two chairs from the kitchen along with the hammer and the box of nails from the tool cupboard.

We have to try twice, because the first time, the curtain wasn't stretched out properly, which created a big dip in the middle. Nonetheless, it was worth the effort: the results are almost identical to what I saw on the YouTube how-to videos I watched.

Stephie asks, "Do you want us to conduct a test? I put on fresh lip gloss in case you wanted to film me."

"We might as well!"

I set up my camera on the tripod and turn my reading lamp toward the curtain. When I say "Action!" my friend immediately starts to recite poetry in a very expressive way.

Yeah, I know! I can't get over that she's able to do that!

8

No Signal in Saint-Joseph-du-Lac

Leaning my head against the window, I watch the landscape go by. We're on the way to Saint-Joseph-du-Lac, on the North Shore of Montréal, to get to one of my dad's favorite orchards. Myriam came to pick us up around nine, without her daughter, Leah. Virgil asked why she wasn't coming with us, and Myriam answered that she was spending the weekend at her best friend's place.

It's pretty chilly, especially with the wind, but it's sunny too. We're crossing the bridges over Rivière des Prairies and Rivière des Mille Îles, and from the back seat of the car, I manage to get a photo of a highway sign that says "Sainte-Thérèse/Rosemère/Bois-des-Filion." I create a group conversation with Sabrina and Clementine, and I send them the pic, along with a message, "I'm in your neighborhood. 😌"

I ask the people in the car, "Is Saint-Joseph-du-Lac close to Bois-des-Filion?"

"Not really," answers Myriam. "The two cities are both on the North Shore, but a good distance apart. Why?"

"Just curious. I know some people who live there."

In truth, I'd have really liked it if Clementine and Sabrina could join us. It's not that I don't feel like spending time with my family (and Myriam), it's mostly just that I want to get closer to other people like me. Apart from Stephie, Liam, and maybe Mael-a, the only ones I really talk to are on the Internet.

My new friends don't seem to be online. Maybe they're still in bed. I glance over at Virgil, who's busy playing his game, and Borki, squished between us. I can't help yawning. I stayed up late on the computer last night, trying to put a picture in place of the lime green curtain in one of the videos I filmed of Stephie. No luck. It's a lot harder than I expected. My dad ended up raising his voice to get me to go to bed, because he knew I could spend the whole night on it if he let me. Especially since, right now, I don't have to get up early to deliver papers anymore like I used to.

I check my YouTube notifications: *The Great Comeback of Dolores von Tragic* has gotten lots of shares and views, but nothing compared to the video Lydia

Dynamite shared on Twitter. There are a few new comments of the same kind as yesterday ("Hahaha!" and "My God!"), and I answer with emoticons. I read online that it was a good idea to interact with people on my channel.

Soon, we pull off the highway to follow a country road. I take a photo of a field with two mountains behind it. With the sun coming out from behind white clouds and lighting the landscape, it's very pretty. I post it on Instagram. I also feel like sending it to Liam, but I'm afraid to bother him. I know he trains on the weekends and I don't want him to find me annoying if I write to him too often. Instead, I send the photo to Stephie. It doesn't bother me if she finds me annoying. Three little dots appear right away, telling me she's in the midst of typing a response, but I don't have time to get it. I let out a little grumble. I had forgotten there's no network in this backwards place. It's such a pain to have to spend the day cut off from the world.

We arrive at the orchard. Borki is so happy, he jumps out of the car and starts running all over the gravel parking lot.

"Just smell that beautiful country air!" my dad says, stretching out.

Virgil takes a too-deep breath and chokes.

At the reception desk, a smiling woman greets us and gives us each a cardboard box to fill. We start walking. My dad, who has specific plans in mind, tells us what kinds of apples to pick. Apparently, there's a real difference between baking a pie with McIntosh apples versus Lobo apples. It's all the same to me, so I go to the trees he points out. Virgil devours more fruits than he picks—he's such a glutton!

My father's in heaven. "Oh, look how beautiful they are over here! Who wants to climb up and pick them? I'm not sure the little ladder will hold the weight of an adult…."

I shrug. "I can do it."

I climb the ladder and pick a few apples, which do seem to be of top quality, before I take my phone out of my pocket to see if I have better luck getting a signal from up high. All in vain; I don't even get the smallest bar!

When I put away my cell, I drop one of the apples. It bounces off a branch and hits Virgil in the head. He picks it up, and says, "Whoa! This one's perfect." He takes a bite as he heads off toward another tree.

I climb down the wobbly ladder slowly and put the fruit I picked into my box. Since everyone's busy elsewhere, I take the opportunity to sit down on the grass for a bit. It's not a race, after all!

Even though I have no Internet access, I can still take pictures. I decide to take selfies with the apple tree behind me. I must be taking too much time on it because Myriam comes to find me, looking worried. "You okay? Not too bored?"

"No, no. It's just that there's no signal here."

"We're far from the city, that's for sure."

She sits next to me and looks at me more closely. "Is something bothering you?"

"I had a big week. Did my dad tell you I'm running in the school election?"

"No, he hasn't mentioned it. Bravo! Actually, he just mentioned that you had gone to the LGBT+ Center drop-in and that you'd come home a little late. He was worried about you!"

"Ah, yes, we went to a café afterward. And I traveled home with Liam."

"Who's Liam?"

I blush. "A guy at my school. We get along well."

"Uh-oh! I get the feeling you're hiding something from me!" Myriam says with a smile.

"I like him a little. But don't tell my dad, he knows his mother!"

Myriam pretends to zip up and lock her mouth. She throws the imaginary key far into the orchard. Then she gets up and brushes off her jeans.

"Anyway, he'll be disappointed to see how few apples you've picked. Go on, get to work!"

She winks at me, then goes off to find my dad and Virgil.

♥ ♥ ♥

Once the boxes are full, mine included, we head back to the car. As he settles into the front passenger seat, my father exclaims, "I think this is the biggest haul we've ever picked in our whole lives. Thanks, Myriam!"

"You're welcome! Thanks for inviting me."

"Anyone here hungry for hot dogs?"

Virgil groans. "My tummy hurts...."

"That's because of the acidity of all the apples you ate. A good greasy meal will get your stomach in order, I'm sure of it!" says Myriam.

We hit the road. I try to get a signal again, but nothing comes up until we've stopped for lunch at a diner near the highway. Suddenly, all the notifications arrive: I have comments on YouTube, new people following me on Instagram, a Messenger message from Samira who wants to know if we're still on for tomorrow, Stephie's response to the photo I sent her ("Ooooh, pretty!"), another one from Sabrina and Clementine asking me what I'm doing in the area, and...several texts from Liam!

> *Hey, Ciel! How's it going?*

> *Want to come over for lunch? I only have training at 1 p.m. today!*

> *I can come over to your place if you prefer, it's on my way.*

> *You must be busy. Sorry to bother you!*

> *Or maybe you're still asleep? Anyway, sorry!*

"Ciel!"

Absorbed in my messages, I don't hear him. My dad raises his voice. "CIEL!"

I look up from my phone, annoyed. "What?"

"It's your turn to order. What do you want?"

"Oh! Uh…a vegetarian cheeseburger and onion rings." I'm not a vegetarian, but I really like veggie burgers. I prefer their texture over the ones with real meat, and they're really flavorful, too!

I look at the time on my phone: it's 12:32. Too late to get lunch with Liam, that's for sure. I hurry to answer him as we make our way toward a picnic table.

> Hey! It's me who's sorry, we went apple-picking at an orchard super far away in the country, and there was no network signal!

I don't even have time to get my cheeseburger before my phone vibrates.

> Phew! I was worried you were mad at me.

> Ha ha! Never.

> I'm on my way to my training.

> We could get together after, if you want?

> Wait, I have an idea.

Liam types for a long moment. The suspense is killing me.

"You're not eating, Ciel?"

The meal has appeared on the table where everyone's sitting. Without looking up from my screen, I sit down and take a big bite of my cheeseburger, which is incredibly delicious for a roadside diner. Liam finally answers.

Sorry, I was in the metro.

My training finishes at 4, but there's free swim after. Want to come join me?

I can't help a big smile from spreading over my face. Myriam notices, and says, "Ah, look! Did someone get good news?"

Virgil, with his mouth full, adds, "I think Ciel has a crush on someone."

I elbow my brother, who's laughing because I'm still smiling.

9

"Ma Demoiselleau"

Back at home, as I wait for Liam to finish his training, I help Virgil peel apples while my dad makes the piecrust. Myriam is busy with the dehydrator, into which she's placing future apple cinnamon chips. Spread out on the kitchen counter are all the ingredients we need to make apple butter.

My hands are all sticky after I'm finished peeling all the apples I had in front of me. Once I've done mine, I go over Virgil's; he always leaves tons of little peel bits here and there, which is not great for pies. I look at my phone: it's three o'clock. I decide to get ready to go meet Liam at the pool.

As usual, I put on my bathing suit under my clothes so I can spend as little time as possible in the changing room. I don't really like getting changed with strangers.

If it had been anyone other than Liam, I'm not sure I'd have agreed to go swimming. I grab my beach towel, which is decorated with characters from the manga *Sailor Moon*, and then I hesitate a moment: Liam might find it juvenile. But since I remember he likes everything to do with cartoons and Japanese culture, I put it in my bag.

To get to the back door that opens onto the balcony where my bike is locked, I need to go through the kitchen. My dad intercepts me.

"Where are you going dressed like that?"

"To meet Liam at his training."

"Are you coming home for dinner?"

"I don't know yet. I'll keep you posted!"

I get on my bike and pedal slowly toward the sports and rec center Liam told me about. It's not far, it's nice out, and I'm early, so I can take my time.

I still get there at three-fifteen. The lady at the desk gives me a look when I open the door, because it's not time for free swim. I feel obliged to explain why I'm here.

"Hi! I'm here to see my friend Liam, who's training right now."

Her face splits into a smile. "Ah yes, our star! You can go have a seat. Samuel's parents are here too."

She shows me a door that leads to the pool bleachers.

The smell of chlorine overwhelms me as soon as I open it. I haven't been to a public pool in years! I'd forgotten how hard it is on the nostrils.

On the side of the pool, I see a tall redhead, who must be the trainer, giving instructions to the swimmers. There are five of them, all teenage boys, but I can't pick Liam out of the bunch. They're too far away and they all look alike with their swimming goggles, bathing caps, and identical swim trunks.

Two adults are also seated at the top of the bleachers. The parents of the aforementioned Samuel, I imagine. I don't feel like meeting them, so I sit on the lowest bench and take out my phone while keeping a distracted eye on what's happening. Under the trainer's guidance, the swimmers are crossing the pool using different strokes. Then they perform stretches in the water. Is this what Liam spends all his time doing?

I see that Stephie sent me a text while I was on the way here.

> *Are we still on for me to come sleep over tonight?*

> *Ah crap! I completely forgot. Liam invited me to come swimming with him!*

Ooh! Lucky! Will you finish late?

Uuuuuuh...I dunno...Maybe?

OK, it's for a good cause. I'll see if Frank is free! 😄

I hope her plan B works. I feel kind of bad for forgetting her.

After a moment, she texts me back:

It's cool, you're getting out of it this time. Frank would rather go to the movies tonight and not tomorrow. Shall we postpone our pajama party to next week?

We didn't talk about a pajama party! Just that you would come sleep over. In the bathtub.

With the spiders.

And the bats.

It'll be so cool! 😍

The swimmers get out of the water. I can finally see which one is Liam, and I wave my arms at him. He doesn't see me, so I say his name loud enough for him to hear. He turns around and walks quickly toward me. He leans against the little barrier that separates the bleachers from the pool and smiles at me. "Hey! How long have you been here?"

"Oh, not long, maybe half an hour?"

"Ha ha! 'Not long?' You really have a strange concept of time. Does that mean you saw me goofing off in the pool?"

"Actually, I was on my phone. But I'm sure it was impressive!"

On his high chair, the lifeguard blows his whistle. Liam takes a step back.

"I have to leave. There's a change of lifeguards, and they have to do tests on the pool before the free swim. We're not allowed to stay here during the procedure. Come meet me at the locker room door!"

He hurries to get out of the lifeguard's line of sight, and I do the same. In the lobby, people are starting to arrive for the opening of free swim. Liam comes out of the boys' locker room, his towel (in team colors) over his shoulder and flip-flops on his feet. He's dripping everywhere. The reception desk clerk protests: "Liam, you troublemaker! You're getting the floor all wet!"

"I'm sorry, Lynn, I won't be long." He turns to me. "Did you have fun at the orchard?"

"Yeah. Now we'll be eating apples for breakfast, lunch, and dinner. On toast, as a snack, for dessert. Sliced on salads, stuffed in turkey, as a topping on pizza. We're going to dream about apples. We're going to turn into apples."

Liam cracks up. "Wow! I can't wait to see that!"

The walkie-talkie on the reception desk makes some garbled sounds. The clerk calls out to the people waiting in front of the locker rooms: "You're good to go in!"

The crowd carries me into the girls' locker room, separating me from Liam. We signal that we'll meet back at the pool.

Changing in a locker room is a particular experience when you're trans. We're always afraid that someone will intercept us to tell us we're not in the right place. In my case, it's true, I'm not in the right place. But since there's no place for people who are neither girls nor boys, I don't have a choice but to use one of the two locker rooms. I greatly prefer the women's.

I find a locker in a corner and change as quickly as possible, avoiding people's gaze. I take my beach towel, stash my backpack in the locker, lock it, and head for the shower. All this in forty-two seconds, max.

When he sees me come out of the locker room, Liam exclaims, "Took you long enough!"

"No way, I was fast as lightning."

He looks me up and down. I worry he's going to comment on my bathing suit, a yellow flowered two-piece with a little skirt, but instead he says, "Your Sailor Moon towel is way cool!"

"You know it?"

"I haven't seen the show, but I've read the mangas!"

"It's the opposite for me! When they came out with the Netflix series, I binge-watched the whole thing with my brother."

As we get in the water, I ask him, "Do you always train here?"

"No, just on weekends. The other days it's at another place, just near Frontenac metro."

"That's a lot of traveling around to manage!"

"Meh, I'm used to it. It's mostly at school that I have a hard time keeping up. It feels like everything moves too fast. When I'm in the water, it's the opposite. It's like time doesn't even exist. Like I'm in a different dimension."

Liam ducks under the water and lets himself sink. I do the same for a few seconds before coming back to the surface.

Deadpan, I ask him, "So, if I understand you right, being a swimming champion makes you a time traveler?"

"No, you don't get it! It means I can communicate with the beyond. You want to talk to a ghost? Turn someone into a zombie?"

Splash! He dives into the water and comes up again, holding his arms out in front of himself zombie-style. "Mmmm, braaainnsss! Nom, nom, nom...."

"Ha ha ha! I bet you couldn't even catch me."

He stops short and looks defiant. "Are you kidding me? You're talking to a swimmer who got a gold medal at nationals!"

"Pff! No big deal. Want to race?"

"That's cheating! I just spent two hours training. I'm beat!"

"All right! One, two, three...go!"

Even though I start swimming before he does, he catches up quickly. In a few strokes, he reaches the other side of the pool, then comes back to the starting point before I even reach halfway. This must be the most awful defeat in the history of humanity.

♥ ♥ ♥

Eventually, Liam invites me to come over for dinner after our swim. He comes home with me so I can drop off my bike and tell my dad, and then we walk to the bus stop.

The bus that goes to Liam's neighborhood arrives just then. Normally, when I take it, it's full of kids yelling and roughhousing, but since it's the weekend, it's almost empty. And there's a free seat!

I ask Liam, "Is your mom home?"

"No, she's giving painting classes all evening."

"Oof, that's a long time. My dad has to take a nap after every three-hour class he teaches!"

"She works in a studio, not at a college. She only has ten students or so. She can spend the whole class painting and not speaking. Her students watch her. I imagine it's less tiring. That's what she would do at home, anyway, so she might as well get paid for it!"

"Does she take part in exhibitions?"

"Not very often. She tries to organize at least one a year, but it's tiring for her. She prefers teaching."

"If I had her talent, I'd want to show my work, that's for sure."

"And you'd invite me and your friends to the opening, you'd give us a glass of champagne or red wine, and we'd talk about stuff that's meaningless, like, 'Ah yes, look at the power of the brushstrokes in this painting, it's quite exceptional, this is Ciel at the peak of their talent!'"

"Ha ha ha! Um, I didn't understand anything you just said."

Liam laughs, then signals the driver to stop. We get off the bus and walk toward his place. I find his home very comforting. Paintings, drawings, and sculptures are scattered everywhere, along with black-and-white photos in pretty frames. Liam's room, as always, is in monumental disarray. While I wait at the doorway, he shoves aside the clothes and books that litter his bed. He comes back to the door and invites me in, making a bow.

"Ma demoiselleau."

"Ma...what?"

"Demoiselleau. 'Mademoiselle' and 'mon damoiseau' put together. I'm doing my best!"

I laugh (and blush a little) as I sit on the bed. Liam sits in front of his computer in the tidiest corner of the room. He pokes around on his usual websites for a few minutes while I play on my phone. This is how it goes every time we go to his place: we take a moment, separately, to do whatever we feel like. Today, though, there's something different in the air. Like a new shyness.

I'm the first to break the silence. "You know what happened with Sabrina at the café on Wednesday? I think I'm going to make a video about it."

Liam turns his chair around and looks at me with interest. "You're going to call out the café?"

"Maybe not call them out, just...talk about it. It's

not okay that a trans person can't use the bathroom she wants to. And even less so in the Village, which is an area that's supposed to be very open to LGBT people. Of all the cafés in Montréal, we should get some peace in that one!"

"I just hope nobody has too much of a hostile reaction."

"I'm not going to declare war, though. We should have the right to talk about this kind of incident without people freaking out and thinking we're trying to cause trouble."

Liam nods, and then adds, "Hey, not to change the subject, but I'm starving! Normally, I eat right after training."

"Sorry, my fault!"

"No worries, I'm the one who invited you to swim."

We head into the kitchen, and Liam suggests we make sandwiches with leftover salads as a side. I'm happy with just a sandwich, while he serves himself generous portions of tabouleh, couscous, and bean salad.

We take all the food into his room to eat. He sets his laptop on the bed and looks on Netflix for a series he's mentioned to me before. It's in Japanese with subtitles. I have a hard time following it, but it's very funny. The drawings may be adorable, but it's not for little kids, the language is pretty crass. The series is fairly short—ten episodes, each ten minutes long—and we watch the whole thing. Liam gets up to stretch and pile our empty plates on his desk.

"Want to watch something else?"

"Yes, yes. Can we make popcorn?"

"For sure!" He walks to the kitchen.

I call out, "You're not taking the dishes with you?"

"Meh, another time. When my mom wonders where all her plates went!"

I laugh. I like how Liam doesn't try to impress me, he's just really nice. While the popcorn pops in the microwave, I send Stephie a text.

> *Guess who's having a dreamy evening with a good-looking boy?* 😎

> *Uh, me? With Frank?*

> *No, me! With Liam!* 😍

> *Woohoo!!!*

> *What movie did you decide to go see in the end?*

> *The new Marvel movie. Except that Frank got the schedule wrong, so now we have to kill a half hour at the theater.*

> *Aww! Good luck. Gotta go, my cute boy's coming back.*

> *OK! Let me know how it goes!* 😊

Liam enters the bedroom and sets down a big bowl of popcorn in front of me. I hurry to turn off my phone screen so he can't see my conversation with Stephie.

Stretching out on the bed, he asks, "What would you like to watch?"

"Whatever, not picky. Go see what's new!"

After reading a dozen synopses, we agree on a horror film. Liam, who clearly has a huge appetite after his training, shovels popcorn in his mouth by the handful. When he realizes he's already snarfed most of what was in the bowl, he pushes the bowl toward me and orders me to take the rest.

The film is pretty cool: the zombies are really scary, and the atmosphere is convincing. I adore the kind of story I can totally dive into, with all my senses on high alert. But what I enjoy even more is watching Liam's reactions. He makes scared noises when the camera shows a zombie, catches his breath in terror when a person is being devoured, and breathes faster when the suspense is at its peak.

Without warning, he screams and grabs my hand. I laugh with pleasure. The hero of the film survives, but Liam doesn't let go of my hand. He's really just so cute! I take the opportunity to snuggle up to him and lean my head on his shoulder. I notice that he's in a cold sweat. The poor guy is terrorized! I feel bad for enjoying the moment so much, while he looks like he'll be traumatized for life.

10

Two Incisive Representatives

When I open my eyes, I see out the window that the sun is high in the sky. I slept like a log. I get up and glance into Virgil's room. He's already up, which is rare. The house is silent; he must have gone to play outside. There's just my dad in the kitchen, correcting exams.

"Good morning, my little groundhog. You slept a long time!"

"Yeah! I think I was really tired."

On the counter, I find a few candy apples with sticks in them. I guess this is what my dad, Myriam, and Virgil had for dessert yesterday, since I can see three are missing from the marks on the parchment paper where they were placed. I take one and go sit in the living room. I can't stop thinking about the evening I spent with Liam. I left when his mom got home, shortly after the horror film ended. It was warm in Liam's room, and I got the impression we could have stayed there a long time, cuddled together on his bedspread. But he was wilting with fatigue, and I didn't want to overstay my welcome. Sylvie invited me to sleep over, but I blushed to the roots of my hair and said I had to go home.

I can't get it out of my head, the feeling of Liam so close to me. I remember how it felt with Eiríkur, my ex-boyfriend. We talked a lot and he liked being with me, but cuddling wasn't really his cup of tea. I think my attraction for Liam is different. I just always want to take him by the hand and nuzzle my face into his shoulder.

Samira texted me this morning to give me her address. As I wait for it to be time to go over, I watch new videos that explain how to digitally alter a background. Based on the advice of an apparently well-known YouTuber, I install a program on my computer. I need to learn how each button works, which takes a long time.

I notice that Stephie is online, so I hurry to call her. When she answers, I say, "Hey! Am I bothering you?"

"No, no. What are you up to?"

"Not much, just about to get ready to go over to Samira's to work on our election campaign."

"Looking forward to it?"

"I dunno. We don't know each other very well, the two of us, and I'm afraid it'll be uncomfortable."

"You shouldn't worry. Everything will be fine. Is that what you wanted to talk about? You're afraid of Samira?"

"No...." I lower my voice so my dad can't hear. "Liam and I held hands!"

"Ooh la la! You're getting serious!"

I get up from my chair and go lie down on the sofa, smiling from ear to ear. "It was so great. We were watching a horror film, there were tons of zombies."

"So romantic!"

"You should have seen him, he was really scared! We stayed cuddled up for the whole movie."

"Ha ha! Too cute!"

"You think it means something?"

"Hmm. Apart from that he's a scaredy cat?"

"Yes, apart from that. Do you think he likes me too?"

"Well, if he held your hand, he's in love with you. Fact."

"Are you sure? Like, sure sure?"

"Pretty much, yes. Either that or he's REALLY a scaredy cat, and that's very cute."

"He is going to be thirteen in a few weeks...."

"Yeah...." There's a small silence, and then Stephie says, "But, now, you really did snuggle?"

"Absolutely, just as I said."

"If I were you, I'd have made a move."

I sigh. "I don't know, Stephie. I'm afraid I'll get it wrong. Sometimes I've mixed up simple acts of familiarity with more serious feelings. You remember in fifth grade when Leo told me he liked my hair, and I spent the rest of the month writing him love letters?"

"At least he just showed them to me, not to the whole class. He didn't know how to tell you to stop!"

"It made me so sad."

Stephie lets out a little sigh. "Yeah, I know. But if I were you, I'd take a chance with Liam. Because if you don't tell him what you're feeling, you'll never know his answer. You could, I don't know, give him a little gift to show him you like him."

"That's an idea. I'm not in a rush, though. I just broke up with Eiríkur. I need some time for myself."

"Eiríkur? You haven't seen him in four months, and it's been a month since he broke up with you!"

"Excuse me, it's been twenty-three days. And you know it takes me some time, this stuff."

"I know, I know," says Stephie in a gentler tone.

I change the subject. "So, how did your night with Frank go yesterday?"

"It went well. The movie was a bit long, though. Hey, you remember how Frank decided to sew a pair of shorts for his personal project for science and tech? Well, he already started tracing the pieces on the fabric the guy at the shop gave him, and he brought the scraps to my place. My mom gave me a little sewing machine for Christmas two years ago, so he can practice with it. I'm so proud of him!"

"Cool! Oh, I gotta go. I'm going to Samira's."

"Okay, bye!"

I hang up, satisfied. Talking with Stephie always puts me back on track.

♥ ♥ ♥

Samira lives on the ground floor of a residential building on Rue de Bellechasse, about ten blocks from me. A woman with long, shiny hair dyed dark red opens the door. I clear my throat, intimidated.

"Hi, I'm here to see Samira."

My classmate pops out behind her and says, "I got it, Dad, this is for me!"

Samira's dad looks at me with a smile. "What's your name?"

"Uh…Alessandra. But you can also call me Ciel."

"Ah yes, you're the one who's running with Samira in the school elections? Congrats! I'm Jolene."

"Pleased to meet you!"

Samira takes me to her room. It really gives the impression of a well-behaved, studious girl. The white walls are covered in posters for bands I don't know. Near the window, there's a desk with a green plant and lots of school supplies, and next to it there's a little bookshelf. A black-and-white shag rug covers the floor. The only thing that doesn't fit is a black vanity with a mirror, strewn with lipsticks and eyeshadow compacts, which surprises me because I've never seen Samira wearing makeup at school. I can see a clear distinction between our tastes: while I prefer bright colors, the makeup on her vanity leans into the darker shades. I didn't picture this side of Samira.

She sits on her bed and invites me to use the desk chair, then pulls a pink portfolio out of her bag. Inside, there are lots of papers and a little black notebook, which she starts flipping through.

"So, I've thought of a game plan, tell me what you think of it. First: target clear electoral promises so our team stands out from Jérôme-Lou's. Second: establish a multi-phase campaign plan."

I interrupt her, a little lost. "Uh, meaning?"

"Meaning we need to show who we are in different ways throughout the campaign. For example, we might plan two or three postering operations, and each one would talk about certain issues to make an impression on people."

"That seems a little complicated…."

"It's just an idea, we'll see. Third: be available to listen to the needs of the LGBT community at Simonne Monet-Chartrand."

"Yeah, well, that goes without saying."

"Not for Jérôme-Lou, though," replies Samira.

I smile. "You're right. But remember we have to sign up with the student life director in order to run in the election."

"Yes, yes, I'll do that tomorrow. Do you want to come with me?"

"Uh…okay."

"Super. So, let's come back to my first point: targeting clear electoral promises. Jérôme-Lou and Marine are relying on their popularity to win. They don't really care about improving students' lives. All they want is to get re-elected. I'm sure we can do better than that!"

"And what would our promises be? Installing TVs in each classroom? A popcorn machine in the cafeteria?"

"No! Actually, I re-watched some of your videos yesterday, and took notes on what you were saying about our school." Samira takes a few loose sheets out of her portfolio. "There was, uh…adopting an inclusion policy for trans and gender-nonconforming students, adding all-gender bathrooms…."

"And you think we can do that if we're elected to run the Alliance?"

"For sure. The position exists for exactly this kind of thing."

All of a sudden, the school election takes on a new importance for me. I'd like to be elected, and not just to help Stephie or please Samira. It's exciting to think we could really make a difference. I hit the desk with my fist. "Well, then we have to win!"

"Now you're talking! I also thought of another point. Did you notice, that apart from you and me, all the other members of the Gender and Sexuality Alliance are white? It totally doesn't represent the proportion of racialized kids at school."

"What do you propose?"

Samira digs into her portfolio again and pulls out a sheet with a flag printed on it.

"We could use this flag throughout our campaign. It's the LGBT rainbow flag, with two stripes added, one brown and one black, to symbolize the inclusion of racialized people."

When I look at the sheet, I remember Bettie Bobbie Barton, the YouTuber who posted a horrible video about me last month, where she suggested I should go back to my own country because I have darker skin. It still doesn't sit well with me.

"You think this would attract more non-white people?"

"I don't know, but anyway, it sends a clear message that with our team, everyone is welcome at the Alliance."

I agree with enthusiasm. "It's a great idea!"

"Yippee!"

We start planning our posters. I manage to convince Samira to keep it to one postering campaign. There are less than two weeks before the vote, after all!

On a page of her book, she sketches out a poster. "Here we'd put a photo of you and me…."

"Are we going to use a funny filter on the pic? Jérôme-Lou and Marine put dog noses on theirs."

"Never!" says Samira, making a face.

"Phew! I was afraid it was mandatory." I say this sarcastically, and Samira laughs before continuing.

"Just below, we can write 'Vote for Samira and Ciel' in big letters."

"Hmm. I don't know if I'm allowed to write Ciel. It's not the name on the attendance sheets and all."

"You think it will be a problem?"

"No idea. On the voting ballot, I might need to use the name the school has on file."

"What would you like to use, in that case?"

I think for a moment, before gesturing for Samira to pass me the book. I write, "Alessandra/o."

"Alessandra is the name the teachers use in class, and Alessandro is what the Ministry of Education has on file. That way, we're sure we won't get it wrong!"

Samira approves. "What do you think of filling it out like this: 'Samira and Alessandra/o to represent the Gender and Sexuality Alliance.'"

"Okay."

Next, we think about a slogan. Samira suggests, "It could be 'Two incisive representatives to make S.M.-C. more inclusive.' S.M.-C. for Simonne Monet-Chartrand, of course."

"Cool, it rhymes! But what does 'incisive' mean?"

"We have a little bite, we pierce through. Like the teeth, incisors, you know?"

"Oh, got it! Perfect. I love the poster!"

"Now we just need to make it for real!"

I pretend to be clueless. "Really? I thought we'd just stick the page from your book up at school."

"Ha ha! With these stick figures? People will have a hard time recognizing us."

"That wouldn't bother me. It's embarrassing, putting pictures of ourselves on the school walls!"

Samira pays no attention and flips her phone camera into selfie mode before pulling me against her and smiling. We have to take a good fifty photos before we're both satisfied with the result. One of us is always blinking, or smiling in a weird way, or we don't like the angle of our noses.

Once we've picked the photo, Samira says, "I'm going to ask my dad or my mom to help me make the poster on the computer tonight. And tomorrow, we can go see the student life director so he can print up a bunch of copies. You think he'll let us do them in color?"

"I hope so! They'll be boring if they're just in black and white."

Samira closes her portfolio and declares our work session finished. I don't want to seem impolite by leaving right away, so I chat with her a bit. We talk about school, our parents, and my YouTube channel. I marvel, "I can't believe you watched all my videos last night!"

"Not all of them. Just the ones that were relevant to school. I came across some funny stuff, though, like your little brother dressed as a drag queen!"

"Ah yes! Dolores von Tragic. An instant classic."

"What will your next video be about?"

I hesitate for a moment before telling her about our misadventure with Sabrina. But knowing that Samira's dad is also trans, I take a chance. "I was thinking of doing one about something I witnessed in a café this week."

I summarize the incident while watching for her

reaction. It turns out I was right to trust her, as she exclaims, "Oh my goodness! That's awful!"

"No kidding."

"So, in the video, you'll explain what happened?"

"Yes, but without naming my friend."

Samira looks thoughtful. "I'd be careful if I were you. With Jolene, my dad, strangers often call her 'sir,' but she hates when we correct them. The situation is already too embarrassing for her. She doesn't want to attract more attention. So, I don't know if your friend would be happy if you talked about her in a video, even without naming her. She might prefer to forget the whole thing."

Samira's argument makes me think. I replay the scene in the café: Sabrina blushing in humiliation, Clementine wanting to yell at the employee, Sabrina hurrying to bring us all outside.... Clearly, she wanted to avoid making a scene.

I bite my lip and say to Samira, "You're right, I hadn't thought of that."

♥ ♥ ♥

On my way home, I send Sabrina a message on Instagram, asking her if she'd mind if I talked about our misadventure in a video. A few minutes later, I get her answer:

Sabrina: Hey! I'd rather not, to be honest.

I'm both relieved that Samira made me think to ask Sabrina's permission before making the video, and disappointed at her refusal. Still, I write back:

Ciel: No problem! I respect your choice.

Sabrina: That's nice of you.

Ciel: Are you coming to the next drop-in?

Sabrina: I'll have to see! I might skip this one. I have a lot of homework.

Ciel: Argh, me too. Actually that's why I'm going, to get my mind off it!

Sabrina: Hahaha!

I don't know Sabrina well, so I can't tell if she's telling the truth or if it's just an excuse to not have to come. I still remember what Liam said to me when we were saying good-bye after the café incident. He had predicted that what happened might make Sabrina lose interest in coming to the meetings. What if he was right? I'd be sad to not see her again because of that.

Since I have the night free, I try to finish my homework early for once. It's pretty hard, because the table is piled with pies and other apple pastries my dad has been baking full-time since yesterday. That's not counting the preserves spread out to cool all the way out into the living room: apple jelly, apple butter, apple compote, apple ketchup, apple jam.... I take a photo of the place and send it to Liam.

Hahahaha! Sick!

Wait, are those mini apple pies I see?!
They look so good!

When he says this, a plan takes root in my head: I could bring him one tomorrow as a gift, like Stephie suggested. Before going to bed, I sneak a tartlet and wrap it in parchment paper, and then I draw little apples on it. I put it in my favorite container, the one with cats with big angry eyes. He'll absolutely have to give it back to me: that will be one more reason to talk with him outside French class.

I put the container in my lunch box. Nobody will be the wiser.

11

Guy's Optimism

The next morning, I run into Samira in the hallway. She stops me and pulls me by the arm over to the lockers, away from where people can see us. She shows me the template for our poster on her phone. Everything's there: the photo, the rainbow flag with the brown and black stripes, and our slogan.

As I study the poster, I comment, "You know what? I'm not sure I like my nose in that picture."

"Too late! Anyway, your nose is perfect."

"I know, I'm kidding. The poster looks great!"

"And it was easy to do! It took me and my dad five minutes."

"I'll hire you for all my future poster needs."

"Thank you, thank you."

We agree to go to the student life office after lunch to sign up as election candidates, and then I go to meet Stephie at our locker. I take the carefully wrapped tartlet out of my lunch box and show it to her.

"It's for Liam. Do you think he'll like it?"

She smiles from ear to ear and cries, "Awwwww, it's so cute! If he can resist that, I don't know what to tell you! With little apple drawings on top of it all…. Oh my God, I'm gonna cry!"

I'm about to tell her not to lay it on so thick, but then I realize she's really feeling it. Must be hormones! Anyway, when Frank joins us, she jumps into his arms as though she hadn't seen him for a century. Which doesn't stop her from following us to our science and tech classroom to ogle Mr. Brazeau.

♥ ♥ ♥

As soon as I arrive at our usual lunch table, Samira hurries to ask if she can show our poster to everyone. I nod. Our friends have only kind words for what we've made. While Samira's phone is being passed from hand to hand, Stephie leans over and whispers in my ear, "Your nose looks funny in that pic."

"Stop! My nose is perfect."

She sticks her tongue out at me and smiles. She's the only person I'd let get away with saying something like that.

Samira asks, "Are there any volunteers to help us put up the posters? We'll have to plaster them all over the school!"

"All over the school?" asks Stephie, surprised. "Isn't that going overboard?"

"That's what Jérôme-Lou did. We need to fight fire with fire."

"I can help put them up," answers Annabelle. "When are we doing it?"

"The sooner the better."

"I can't do it after class today."

Samira looks at me, and I suggest, "In that case, we can do it before class tomorrow."

Stephie and Annabelle agree to meet us in the agora tomorrow half an hour before classes begin, but Zoe and Felicia explain that they can't get in earlier in the morning.

Samira waits impatiently for me to finish eating my bag of apple chips so we can go see Guy, who's in charge of student life.

"Come on, Ciel, hurry up!" says Samira. "We have to sign up today. I wouldn't want us to be turned down as candidates because we got started too late."

I try to calm her down. "No, no, don't worry. I'm sure Guy will let us sign up."

"I just want to get it done." She tells me to finish my apple juice as we walk.

I decide not to push back, given how worked up she seems to be, so I gather up my things (taking care not to tip over the container with the tartlet in it) and follow her obediently to the student life office. It's located at the very back of the cafeteria, in the same hallway as the nurse. When we get there, we see that Guy is deep in discussion with an older student. We wait for our turn. Samira can't stop biting her nails.

Once the student leaves, we enter the office, which is buried in posters, photos, trophies, and other souvenirs Guy has collected over time—he says he's worked here for more than twenty years.

He greets us warmly. "Ah, my friends! Come in, come in! Pull up a chair. How can I help you?"

Samira speaks up. "We want to run in the school elections."

"That's fabulous! I love it when young people get involved. It totally rocks, as you say! All you need is your student card. What committee do you want to represent?"

Samira glances my way. I understand that it's my turn to speak.

"For the Gender and Sexuality Alliance."

Guy freezes and looks at us, seeming not to understand. "The Gender and Sexuality Alliance? Are you sure?"

"Yes."

"Didn't you know? Jérôme-Lou and Marine are running again this year!"

Samira smiles at Guy. "Oh, we know!"

There's a short, embarrassed silence before he responds. "Right. Um, well, I'll just say this right away then—it's no big deal if you lose. It can be humiliating, of course, but that's part of the democratic process."

"You're so optimistic," replies Samira sarcastically.

"Realistic, more like! Jérôme-Lou will be re-elected, without a shadow of a doubt. He's very popular."

I ask, "Can we...can we still run?"

Guy seems a little mixed up. He takes our student cards, mumbling, "Yes, of course, of course...." He types out the information on our cards. "And who would be the president?"

Samira raises her hand. "Me."

"And I'll be the vice-president."

Guy turns back to us and clears his throat before saying, "Perfect, you're registered. Do you have any questions?"

Samira pulls a USB key out of her pocket and holds it out to him. "Yes, actually, we wondered if you could print out copies of our poster."

Guy scratches his chin. "I can sign a permission slip for you to use the printing center. It's normally just for teachers, but I can make an exception. You can use the printer there."

"That's very kind, thanks! Does it print in color?"

"No, sadly, only in black and white."

Samira points at the printer sitting on Guy's desk. "That one, then?"

"Oh! That's my personal printer. It prints in color, but it would be cheating if I let you use it."

Samira opens her mouth to protest, but I hurry and answer first. "Too bad. We'll use the printing center then!"

Guy scribbles an authorization note and we say thanks and leave.

♥ ♥ ♥

"We were able to print thirty copies of the poster. Samira kept them. She's going to add the rainbow flag colors by hand tonight. She insisted, and I'm not very good at drawing, so...."

Liam sits with his arms crossed over the desk we

share in French class and listens to me give the rundown of our meeting with Guy.

"Do you need help putting up the posters?" he asks.

"No, it should be fine. We'll take care of it tomorrow morning."

"Okay. If I can do anything, just let me know!"

"You're too kind! Hee hee."

I wanted to look cute by giggling at the end, but instead a weird squeak comes out of my mouth. I'm probably too nervous because of the tartlet. I plan to give it to him at the end of class. That way, he won't feel obliged to eat it in front of me and he won't think I was in a hurry to give it to him. And I know myself—I wouldn't dare look at him for the rest of class if I gave it to him now.

During the whole first part of the class, I think about an offhand way to give him my gift. "Oh, before I forget—here, I brought you a surprise."

Destiny had something else in mind, though. Mrs. Walter hands out an exercise sheet that needs to be done in teams of two. Liam turns to me and says, "I'm so hungry, I can't stand it. I'll never be able to focus!"

I can't help myself. My hands grab my lunch box, and my vocal cords kick into gear without my consent. "Funny enough, I brought you something! Would you like an apple tartlet?"

Let's remember this was supposed to be a surprise. He was supposed to open the container and see what's inside.

Still, he's happy when I extend the container to him with a trembling hand. He exclaims, "Oh! You didn't need to. Thank you!"

At least he seems to appreciate my gesture. He comments on my little drawings on the parchment paper that holds the pastry, and he swallows the tartlet in two big bites, which sends pastry crumbs flying all down his navy blue hoodie. He tries to shake them off, but it's useless. He has to scratch at the fabric with his nails to dislodge the crumbs.

"That was delicious. Say thanks to your dad from me!"

"You're welcome!" I say, disconcerted.

"Uh, thanks to you also, of course."

"Huh? Oh, no, I didn't mean to say 'you're welcome!' Well—I mean, I didn't want you to feel you had to thank me too. Just my dad, that's cool. After all, he's the one who made the tartlet."

Liam looks at me, visibly amused. He scoops up the crumbs from the table and drops them in the dish before closing the lid. "Here, your container."

"Don't worry, you can give it back to me later."

"You…you want me to wash it?"

I freeze, before understanding that my plan is totally off the rails. I take my dish out of Liam's hands, while babbling, "Not at all! I had just forgotten you'd already eaten the tartlet. I thought you'd take it home, that's all."

"Oops! I guess not, ha ha! I was too hungry, seriously."

"Yeah. So, uh, should we do our work now?"

I turn my attention toward the exercise sheet our teacher handed out. Wow, I really have a knack for sabotaging my own ideas.

♥ ♥ ♥

"I'm sure you were super cute. Maximum adorableness. Liam must have been totally charmed!"

Well, my plan with Liam might have been spoiled, but at least it makes for a great anecdote to tell Stephie. She started out by making fun of me, before softening when she saw my awkwardness.

It's early in the morning, and we're going to meet Samira and Annabelle, who are waiting for us with the posters.

I sigh, and say, "He mostly just didn't seem to be getting what I was saying."

"He liked the tartlet, that's what counts!"

We're arriving at the agora, which is just below the cafeteria. Normally, it's loud and full of people, especially fourth- and fifth-year students, and I try to avoid it as much as possible. But at this time of day, it's empty, and the silence makes the space feel a lot more welcoming.

When she sees us approaching, Samira points at a poster on the wall and exclaims, theatrically, "Have you seen this?"

Stephie and I get closer and see that it's a poster for Jérôme-Lou's election campaign. On the photo, the Alliance president is standing next to his loyal Marine, with their Snapchat dog-nose filter. Under the photo in big letters, the poster reads "VOTE FOR JÉRÔME-LOU," and then "and Marine" in lower-case. The only other things on the poster are *#LAmourGagneToujours*, *#LoveWins*, *#LoveIsLove*, and *#LAmourCEstLAmour*.

Stephie protests, "How are these hashtags even relevant?"

"Ugh, so ridic!" adds Annabelle.

Samira, standing a ways away, adds, "It gets worse! Don't you see?"

"It's a Snapchat filter that's gone out of style and doesn't look very professional?" Stephie guesses, wrinkling up her nose.

"Not just that! Look, compare them to our posters."

I look again and answer right away. "Ours are black and white, theirs are in color."

"Exactly! And I had to spend the whole night coloring rainbows to add color to ours! So frustrating."

"Well, one of them might have access to a color printer at home."

"Pff! I'm sure Guy let them use his personal printer. Ciel, do you remember how he was trying to discourage us from running in the election? And how he kept repeating that Jérôme-Lou and Marine were going to win?"

"Jérôme-Lou is clearly a bootlicker when it comes to Guy," adds Stephie.

"It's favoritism! It's not fair!" gripes Samira.

I answer, "It's impossible to prove, though. Can you picture us interrogating Jérôme-Lou or Guy about it?"

Samira sighs, and pulls two rolls of tape out of her bag along with her pink portfolio, which contains our posters.

"We'll split into teams of two. One person to hold the posters in place, the other to tape them. We'll mostly aim for common spaces, but let's avoid putting too many in the locker wing, since they're more likely to be torn down there. Stephie and Ciel, you take the first floor; Annabelle and I will take the second. We'll meet back here when we're done. Sound good?"

I smile. "Sounds good!"

♥ ♥ ♥

The postering operation went well. As I walked around the school, I noticed that a number of other committees had begun their campaigns: I saw candidates for the environment committee, the cultural activities committee, the newspaper committee, and the Dungeons and Dragons committee (most of the students in the photos were wearing armor or elf costumes!).

It's a funny feeling to walk down a hall and see my own face on the walls. I'm having a hard time getting used to it. I wonder if the students looking at me are connecting me with the poster, or if they're just blown away by my style, which I'm rocking today. I have to say that my iridescent jacket (my dad calls it my "unicorn skin") turns heads, and the overalls I'm wearing under it suit me really well.

In the afternoon, Mael-a intercepts me as I'm on my way to music class. They say, "Ciel! I was looking for you. First, congrats on the campaign! It's so cool that you're running. I'll vote for you, for sure."

"Oh, thanks, but we haven't won yet! Jérôme-Lou is very popular."

"We'll see. I know you'd be a great representative."

"Actually, it's Samira, my teammate, who'll be president. I would be vice-president."

"I still hope you win. Actually, do you have a couple of minutes? I wanted to talk to you about something."

"Uh, sure, yes!"

I'll never get used to older students paying attention to me, not even Mael-a. I'm twice as nervous about saying something stupid or seeming lost. I wait a bit nervously for them to explain what they want.

"You know Armand, the coordinator of the Montréal LGBT+ Center? He was approached by a journalist who wants to do a story on youth. She wants to interview trans youth who are involved in the community. Armand asked me to take part, and he asked if you'd be interested too. The journalist would ask you questions about the drop-in, but you could also talk about your YouTube channel and the school elections. All you need is written permission from one of your parents."

I have to make a huge effort not to seem too excited by what Mael-a is suggesting. I don't want to seem immature. But at the same time, I don't want them to think I'm bored at the idea. The truth is, I'm extremely flattered that Armand thought of me. I answer, "Yeah, I'm interested! I'll talk with my dad about it. When and where would it happen?"

"We're meeting on Saturday at noon at La Brûlerie du Village, on Sainte-Catherine."

"Perfect!"

12

Breaking News: Ciel is Adorable!

"Look the journalist in the eyes. Unless you're being allowed to read the article before it's published, make sure you give short, precise answers, or you could be misquoted."

Leaning against the lockers before our last class of the day, Stephie has been listing off advice for a good five minutes. When I spoke to her about the interview I've been asked to give, she seemed really happy for me. Of course, she's used to journalists because of her mom, who's often on TV. Stephie has also been on TV once or twice. First, when she took part in a documentary on Télé-Québec, then when her video against the bullying of trans people at school went viral, and lastly when she won the national spelling competition. She's become a real pro. That's why she decided to prep me for Saturday's meeting.

"One last thing," she adds. "If she asks you questions about what's in your pants, only answer with a joke."

I don't feel very reassured by the idea.

"This all scares me. I'm not sure I'll be able to remember everything you said."

"Oh, it will go well. You just need to be very nice to her. You could even bring her gifts!"

"Gifts? Like what?"

"One of your election posters, for example. Where will the interview be happening?"

"At a place called La Brûlerie du Village."

"That's not the café where your friend was insulted, I hope?"

"Uh…,I don't think so."

Truth be told, I don't remember the name of that place. Me and my goldfish memory….

♥ ♥ ♥

Once I'm back home, I send Clementine an Instagram message to ask if she remembers the name.

Clementine: It was Café Mousseux. Why? You want to speak out against the employee?

Ciel: No, I'm meeting a journalist Saturday in a café in the Village, and I wanted to make sure it wasn't the same place.

Clementine: You're meeting a reporter?! Too cool! What's the occasion?

I summarize what Mael-a told me. Clementine seems very enthusiastic, and says she'll look for the article when it comes out.

At that moment, my dad comes into the apartment. I tell him the news about the interview right away. He promises he'll write the authorization letter after dinner. Looking impressed, he says, "An interview in the paper! You're going to be a star! We'll see your face everywhere!"

Suddenly, that idea makes me feel anxious. "You think? I hope I won't look stupid...."

"You'll be perfect, my dear."

Virgil hears our conversation and decides to insert himself. "Can I come?"

I ruffle his hair. "You're too young, Virgil."

"Okay, but could Dolores von Tragic come?"

I smile. I almost want to say yes as I picture the scene: in the metro, me and my little brother, dressed as the diva heiress to a canned tuna empire, going to meet a reporter in a café. But I stay firm. "No. You're too little."

He leaves, grumbling that he's "not that little," and it makes me a bit sad.

♥ ♥ ♥

The next day, in French class, Liam asks me hopefully, "Did you bring me another tartlet today?"

I'm surprised at his question, and a little disappointed he didn't catch on that it was supposed to be a love message.

"No, sorry! I should have, you like them more than I do."

"Ha ha! It was a joke. Don't worry about it."

I try to laugh a little, though my heart's not in it. To change the subject, I announce, "Hey, you'll never guess what Mael-a asked me yesterday!"

"What?"

"They want me to meet with a journalist on Saturday to talk about my community involvement!"

"Whoa! Congratulations. Are you excited?"

"It's a little stressful; I've never done this. What was it like for you, being interviewed, when you won the Canadian junior swimming nationals?"

Liam looks stunned for a moment, then says, "Oh, yeah, that's true. I had forgotten."

"You'd *forgotten*? It was barely a month ago!"

"Well, I didn't get to say much. They just took lots of photos of me. It was a bit annoying, there were so many people!"

"Oh yeah? At least on Saturday there will be just the reporter, Mael-a, Armand, and me."

The bell rings, and our teacher starts the class. Today, I concentrate really hard to listen. Even though I'm no good at French, I really like Mrs. Walter. She's nice and very patient with me.

A few minutes later, Liam makes me jump when he taps me on the shoulder. He slides a piece of paper in front of me. He's drawn a newspaper with a person on the front page: it's me, with a big smile and flowers all around me. Above it, he wrote, "Breaking news: Ciel is adorable!" I can't help grinning as widely as the picture he's drawn of me. "Ciel is adorable!" he wrote. I feel like I'm going to faint from happiness. Trying to be subtle, so that Mrs. Walter doesn't notice, I draw a terrible portrait of Liam next to it and add a caption: "Liam establishes the world record for being the boy who sucks up the most!" before sliding the sheet back toward him. Without looking at him, I hear him snort like he's trying to hold back from laughing. Mrs. Walter turns toward us. I compose a serious face right away, even though right now I'd rather be doing a little tap dance. Liam's little note has filled me with so much hope!

I would have liked to keep the note, but Liam puts it away with the rest of his things. We part ways at the bell when he leaves to eat lunch at home. I meet Stephie at the locker, skipping the whole way.

"My God, you're in a good mood today."

"Guess who thinks I'm adorable?"

"I don't know, your dad?"

"Liam!" I explain what happened in French class.

Stephie seems perplexed. "He drew a caricature of you and wrote that you're adorable?"

"Not a caricature! It was a nice drawing, I had big soft eyes like in a manga, and super nice hair. You should have seen it."

"I should have, definitely. Next time, take a picture!"

We head for the cafeteria. Once we're seated at our table, I tell the girls that I'm going to be interviewed on Saturday, and I say that I'll take the opportunity to mention the election campaign. Everyone at the table is excited, especially Samira, who goes starry-eyed. "That's so cool!"

"I'm sure the reporter will love you," adds Zoe. "You're funny and nice!"

"Don't forget to dress nice, in case they take your photo!" suggests Felicia.

"Ciel never dresses badly. It's just not possible," comments Annabelle with a smile.

The girls move on to compare their respective styles, and they start having fun imagining how they'd dress if they were going to be in the paper.

Samira says to me, "Anyway, with this, we have some chance against Jérôme-Lou!"

♥ ♥ ♥

After lunch, I have my science and tech class with Frank. When the bell sets us free, all the students get up, making noise and commotion. As Frank gathers up his things, he turns to me. "Hey, I never asked whether it worked out with your green curtain, in the end."

"Not really. It's pretty complicated. And with the school elections, I haven't had time to work on it."

"I was talking about it with my big sister randomly yesterday. She's studying graphic design. She said she'd be happy to show you how!"

"Wow, that's so nice of her!"

I'm happy that someone can help me with my project, even though I'm a bit shy about the idea of going to Frank's place for the first time. We're not especially close.

"You can come by tonight, if you want. I have

nothing on after dinner," adds Frank. "I'll give you my address."

I try to mask my uncertainty and I answer quickly. "Cool, thanks! How's your project going? Stephie told me you'd spent a lot of time at her place working on her sewing machine."

"Yeah, not bad. It's hard, but it's super interesting!"

Stephie pokes her nose in the doorway, looking for us. We go meet her. She says, "My class was just nearby, I figured I could come wait for you!"

I crack up. "Sure, that's it! I think you just wanted to see the handsome Mr. Brazeau."

"Uh-oh! You've seen through me like I'm a Ziploc bag."

Her boyfriend coughs, pretending to be offended, and then all three of us crack up.

♥ ♥ ♥

Frank opens the door when I ring his bell, on the second floor of a residential building on Rue Saint-Zotique.

"Hey, Ciel! Did you get my text about the videos?"

He had written to me just before I left my place, letting me know I should bring the videos I'd filmed using the green curtain. His sister needs them to run some tests.

"Yeah, yeah, I have everything I need," I say, showing him my USB key.

As we cross the living room, I see his two younger sisters, one with a coloring book and one reading on the sofa with headphones on. I don't know their names; Frank and Stephie have surely already mentioned them, but I have a terrible tendency to forget that sort of thing.

We cross paths with his mother as she comes out of the kitchen. She says hello, distractedly, and keeps going. I imagine Frank's parents must have become a little blasé over time. Frank invites a lot of friends over—his soccer teammates, Viktor and his gang, Stephie.... At my place, it's a whole event when I invite someone over other than Stephie.

I clear my throat. "Is your big sister here?"

"Yeah, she's expecting us. Before going to see her, do you want to see my project?"

"Sure!"

I follow him to his room. It looks like any teenage boy's room: a bed, a few posters on the walls, a desk where a PC sits, and a lot of clothes strewn on the floor near an empty clothes hamper. I notice, near the window, an old poster of a soccer player, probably someone famous. His guitar is tucked behind the door. I suspect he may have bought it to impress Stephie. I've heard him play a few times, he's not bad.

Frank picks up a bag from the floor and dumps its contents on the bed. It's the fabric the store clerk gave him but cut into all sorts of strange shapes. Frank shows them to me one by one, explaining, "This is the left leg of the shorts; that's the right one. I still have to add this pocket, here, on the left leg. This is supposed to be for the zipper, but it looks complicated, so I might skip that step and just sew on a button, I'm not sure yet. These are the pieces for the waistband."

He looks at me, proud of himself. "So? What do you think?"

"It's super cool. I know nothing about all this, but you seem to know what you're doing."

Truth be told, I'm very impressed that Frank wants to learn to sew. Especially since, if I understand correctly, his parents aren't really encouraging him on this project. Stephie told me they don't think a boy should be interested in sewing.

"Thanks. Okay, want to go see my sister?"

"Sure. What's her name, again?"

"Roula."

I follow Frank into the next room. He knocks before entering and introduces me right away. "Roula, this is Ciel, the friend I was talking about."

His sister is sitting on her bed, holding a magazine.

"Hi, Ciel!" she says. "Did you bring your videos?"

"Yeah," I say, a little intimidated. Roula drops her magazine, gets up, and sits down at her desk and turns on her laptop.

"So, like Frank told you, I'm studying graphic design—not animation or video-making, but in one of my classes we're learning to use a program that's also used to edit films."

I come closer so I can see the screen. She clicks on a tab, and a familiar screen appears. I comment, "That's the same program I downloaded on the weekend!"

"Perfect! Now, I need your USB key."

I hold it out to her, and Roula plugs it into her computer. I show her what file to open. A short video plays of Stephie looking at the camera and making faces. Roula turns to Frank and asks, "Isn't that your girlfriend?"

Frank rolls his eyes. "Oh, boy."

Roula smiles, then explains, "Okay, so what we want is to be able to select the green screen on each image of the video at the same time. You see, all the images are here...."

She selects one, then uses one of the tools on the left-hand toolbar and moves it over to the green screen. "Are you following? Now, we click on the 'Insert' tab, then on 'Background element.'"

A screen appears, allowing Roula to choose a file to download. She selects one, and the green screen disappears. She plays the video again. Stephie's still there making faces, but this time, she's doing it in front of a cat that's playing with a raccoon. Roula leans back in her chair and cracks her knuckles, satisfied.

Amazed, I shout, "Sick!"

13

The Pros and Cons of Going Out with Me

I adore the warm ambiance at La Brûlerie du Village as soon as I step inside. All the furniture is wooden, the lighting is low, and a wonderful hot-chocolate smell floats in the air. I quickly look around to find the little group I'm meeting. Thanks to Mael-a's blue hair, which acts like a beacon in the dark, I find the table right away. As I approach, they wave me over. Armand and a blonde woman wearing glasses, whom I assume is the journalist, turn and greet me in a friendly way.

The woman gets up and introduces herself. "You must be Alessandra! My name is Melinda."

She seems very nice, if a bit reserved. But her tone bothers me a bit. She's talking to me as if I was a child.

"Pleased to meet you! You can just call me Ciel in the article."

She shakes my hand vigorously. Before I can sit down, she points at the café counter. "Would you like something to drink or eat? The paper is treating!"

I look at the table and notice only three cups. I have room in my belly for a snack, but I would feel weird being the only one eating. So I just ask for a strawberry milkshake, which Melinda goes to order at the counter. I sit down next to Mael-a and ask, "I'm not late, I hope?"

"No, not at all. We only just arrived!"

"Phew! Actually, before I forget...."

I open my backpack and pull out my dad's authorization letter. I hold it out to Armand, who answers, "You can leave it on the table, it's for Melinda."

She comes back just then, and as she sits down, she says, "Your milkshake will be ready in a few minutes. If you don't mind, let's get started."

She takes my dad's letter and reads it before tucking it in her purse, and then pulls out a notebook and recorder.

"Are you all comfortable if I record the interview? It won't be broadcast, it's just to help me write the article, so I don't get anything wrong."

We all nod. My stomach feels a bit knotted up. I feel both excited and nervous about what comes next. Melinda presses a red button on the little device and asks us to give our full names. Armand, Mael-a, and I each do so in turn.

While Melinda is going over her notes, the café server comes over and sets down a magnificent pink milkshake, crowned with a red and white straw, just like in the movies. With the other hand, he places a toasted panini in front of Mael-a, and they bite in with gusto. A string of melted cheese falls onto the plate. It looks delicious! I regret not ordering a meal after all.

Melinda clears her throat and begins. "Armand Blouin-Levasseur, to begin, tell me about the youth program at the Montréal LGBT+ Center. What is the organization's mission?"

"With pleasure, Melinda."

Armand's smiling attitude contrasts with the reporter's, which is more serious and a bit pinched. You can tell he's used to working with teenagers: he's funny and relaxed. He quickly explains why the youth program exists, and the kinds of activities he organizes. The journalist then turns toward me and Mael-a.

"Mael-a Saint-Onge and Ciel Sousa, can you tell me about yourselves? What made you want to get involved in the community?"

Mael-a watches me take a long sip of milkshake at that very moment and takes it as a sign to speak first.

"My name is Mael-a. I use the pronoun 'they,' because I identify as non-binary, meaning as neither a boy nor a girl. I'm interested in social justice, which is why

I'm part of the environment committee as well as the Gender and Sexuality Alliance at my school. As well, I decided to volunteer at the Montréal LGBT+ Center to try to make a difference in the lives of young people like me. Before coming to the youth program, I felt like I was alone in the world, because I didn't know anyone who was like me. My parents didn't understand me. Two years ago, I was diagnosed with depression. It was really hard to climb out of it. I don't know how I would have managed if it weren't for the help of the Center volunteers. Now that I'm doing better, I help other young people in turn. This way, I can give back to the community that saved me."

Mael-a's confidence seems to have really affected everyone. Melinda is smiling but seems really moved, with sadness in her eyes, while Armand, his eyes filled with tears, blows his nose on the table napkin that came with Mael-a's panini. As for me, I can't help wondering if I should really be at this interview. Why am I here, except for my YouTube channel where I mostly post silly videos, and a school election that I'm running in only reluctantly to make Samira happy? Mael-a has real reasons to be here, reasons that I knew nothing about until now.

Mael-a, with a casual air, bites into their sandwich, and a big "crunch" fills the silence that follows their story. The reporter adjusts her glasses and looks at me with a kind smile. I take a deep breath and begin.

"Well, I'm just a participant at the drop-in. I've been attending since I was twelve, the youngest allowable age. I'm in my first year of high school and, uh, I'm running with my friend in the school elections for the Gender and Sexuality Alliance."

I take a copy of the poster Samira made out of my backpack and give it to the journalist, as Stephie said I should. Melinda thanks me and I continue.

"Oh, and I have a YouTube channel, but it's nothing very important."

Mael-a interrupts me. "Nothing important? Come on! Your videos, where you call out problems at our school, are incredible! They have a huge impact in making people think and in giving a voice to people like us. Even your silly videos where you're just goofing around, they help because they show that we, too, are allowed to have fun! That our lives aren't just melodramatic stories like the ones you see on TV or in books. It's crucial for people like us to have our own platforms!"

Wow! I had never seen things from that perspective. I feel so happy and proud. Tears fill my eyes and suddenly, there we are: everyone around the table is crying.

♥ ♥ ♥

The interview lasts another fifteen minutes or so, and then Melinda says we need to take some pictures. She waves at a tall man with a shaved head who arrived a bit later, beckoning him to come over. Following his instructions, Armand, Mael-a, and I pose, pretending to be having an animated conversation. Since we feel a bit ridiculous, we end up laughing for real.

Once Melinda and the photographer leave, we stay for a while to discuss the experience.

"Well, I'm looking forward to reading it!" Mael-a exclaims enthusiastically.

"Do we know when the article will be coming out?"

"Monday is a holiday because of Thanksgiving, so it will go out Tuesday, according to what Melinda told me," Armand tells us as he puts on his coat.

We leave the café and head toward the metro. Stopping in front of the LGBT+ Center, Armand turns toward Mael-a and me.

"See you on Wednesday?"

"Yeah!" we answer together.

Mael-a and I walk together to Beaudry station. Before parting ways, we exchange contact information and have a long hug. It feels good, after sharing so many emotions.

When I get home, I hurry to tell my dad all about it. He's thrilled. But it's not enough, so I decide to text Liam. Unfortunately, he can't talk for long because he's going to his training. So, I reach out to Stephie next.

> Just got back from the interview!
> It was awesome!

> I'm happy for you!

> Hey! Didn't we say we'd spend an evening together? You could tell me about it in person!

> Good idea! Wanna sleep over?

> I'll get dressed, grab my things and come over!

I burst out laughing. It's nearly two o'clock. What is she still doing in her pajamas? I know she likes to sleep in on weekends, but this is a bit much!

An hour later, she rings the doorbell. I invite her inside and drag her into my room, super excited to tell her everything.

"…And after that, Mael-a and I exchanged contact info. I'm friends with someone in fourth year!"

Sitting cross-legged on my bed, Stephie smiles, and then frowns. "That's cool, but I'm a bit worried about the photos. The photographer didn't show you any of them?"

"No, but it doesn't bother me. We made the journalist cry! Can you imagine?"

"I admit, that's a feat."

My friend seems to think we've finished with the topic, because she stretches out her legs and says, "What would you say to polishing my toenails?"

"What, can't you do it yourself?"

"It's not that I can't do it, it's that you're super good at it!" she answers, making puppy dog eyes.

"Yeah, yeah. You're lucky I'm so nice!"

"Oh, absolutely!"

I go get my nail polish collection while Stephie pulls off her socks. She chooses the palest pink I have, and I pick a pretty metallic green.

"So, how are things progressing with Liam?" Stephie asks as I bend over her feet.

I lift my head. "What do you mean, 'progressing?'"

"You know, your romance. Has nothing happened since Liam wrote a fake headline saying you're adorable?"

"Well, no…."

"Anyway, I think you should show him more clearly that you're into him. It looks like it'll take forever if you wait for him to say it first."

"Yeah. What should I do, do you think?"

"Hmm, you could…pay an airplane pilot to write 'I love you, Liam' in smoke across the sky. Or you could write it on a giant banner and hang it in the cafeteria."

"Oh my goodness. I would be so embarrassed if someone did that for me."

"Ha ha ha! Me too."

When I finish polishing her toenails, she does mine, and then we attack our fingernails. This activity always relaxes me, as well as bringing back happy memories. In fact, this is what Stephie and I did the first time I went over to her place in fourth grade. At the time, I hadn't yet told anyone I was trans, and people thought I was a boy. It really blew me away when she offered to paint my nails, and that's what marked the beginning of our friendship.

After dinner (apple roast pork with apple fries), I suggest to Stephie that we watch the video I edited with Roula's help this week.

When she sees herself making faces in front of a cat and a raccoon, she groans with her teeth clenched. "I'm warning you, if you show this to Mr. Brazeau, I'll cut you into tiny pieces with a cheese grater!"

"No, no! Now that I've learned how to do it, I can use any other background."

Since I'm handing in my personal project next week, we make a series of videos in front of my green curtain, each one sillier than the last, using everything that we can get our hands on, including my old Barbie dolls that were gathering dust in the closet. We could have kept going till late at night, but Stephie is laughing so hard she can't speak anymore, and we have to take a break. So we stretch out on the bed and gossip about our classmates until sleep takes over.

♥ ♥ ♥

On Sunday, Stephie spends the morning with us playing Wii with Virgil, who's thrilled that my best friend is finally paying attention to him. During this time, I look at memes on the Internet, answer comments on my YouTube channel, and text Liam, whom I hadn't finished telling about my adventure with the journalist.

To Virgil's great chagrin, Stephie has to leave around noon because Frank needs her sewing machine to finish his personal project. I decide to work on mine, too. I pick the best video we filmed yesterday, edit it, and change the background. I resist the temptation to post it on my channel, because I want it to be a surprise for everyone in my class.

Now I have to prepare my oral presentation to explain my process. Mr. Brazeau was very insistent about the importance of citing the sources we consulted. So, I go find the links to some of the YouTube videos I watched, I look up some information on the software I used, and I mention Frank's sister, whom I cite as an expert. To cap it all off, I mention the salesman at the fabric store, even though I no longer remember his name.

I write my text pretty slowly because I can't stop thinking about what Stephie said to me yesterday about "making progress" in my romance with Liam. I'm a little at a loss. I had asked Eiríkur to go out with me, just like that, without really preparing for it. Things were very simple, as I saw it. But with Liam, it's different: I get tons of butterflies in my stomach just from thinking about asking him to be my boyfriend.

It's only the next night, Thanksgiving Monday, that a light bulb suddenly goes off: I'll write him a letter! It will be much less embarrassing that way. I can give it to him after class, and he can read it in front of me or as he walks home, whatever he prefers. It will be perfect.

I have to write ten rough drafts before I find a way of saying it that doesn't come across as too serious, so as not to scare him off. If he doesn't want to go out with me, I still want us to stay friends!

It goes like this:

Liam,
I think you're the coolest guy in the world.
Actually, there's just one thing that would be cooler than you, and that's if we went out together.

Pros of going out with me: you would get lots of tartlets, I smell good, I'll never be better than you at swimming, I have a dog.

Cons of going out with me: people would probably be jealous.

I hope you'll consider all this and come to a favorable decision!

Sincerely,
Ciel 🖤

I decide to decorate the letter with little drawings, since I remember that Liam liked the ones I did on the tartlet wrapping paper. I look for an envelope in our supply closet, but no luck. I end up taking one from my dad's office supplies. I write "Liam" on it, in my best calligraphy, and then I put the envelope with the letter in my backpack so I don't forget it. Phew! I'm tired, as if this whole operation had drained all my energy. I go to bed feeling both happy and anxious.

14

Confession in the Park

When I open my eyes on Tuesday, two minutes before my alarm rings, I'm so dizzy at the idea of telling Liam my feelings for him today that I almost forget the news article is coming out. When I turn on my phone, I see I've already gotten a number of Instagram notifications. People have taken pictures of the front page of the newspaper, where you can see us—Armand, Mael-a, and me—under the big headline, "LGBTQ+ Youth: Getting involved to make a difference." To my great relief, the photo isn't bad. I'm sure my smile looked better at other points in the shoot, but this is probably the shot in which all three of us look the most natural. I can't wait to see the real article! My excitement makes me bounce out of the bed.

I fling open my closet doors and stand in front of

them, hands on my hips. After thinking about it, I decide to wear my favorite outfit to celebrate this big day. I have quite a lot of colorful clothing, but this one breaks all the boundaries: a top with a print of ice-cream cones, rainbow striped socks that go all the way up my thighs, and pale turquoise shorts. A kangaroo sweatshirt with a cloud print on the back adds a casual touch, which makes me think of Liam. He won't be able to resist me!

Once I'm ready to dazzle the whole world, I hurry to show the photo of the front page to my dad, who congratulates me and ruffles my hair.

"Get me a copy of the paper! Oh, and another one to send to your grandmother in Brazil. She'll be so pleased!" He pauses then adds, "Great outfit, by the way. You're radiant!"

"Thanks, Dad!"

After having a quick breakfast, I go outside and get on my bike. It feels a lot warmer out than it has been in the last few weeks, unless it's just euphoria throwing off my body temperature! Whatever it is, I end up taking off my sweatshirt before I melt. I take a detour to the metro station to pick up a few copies of the paper. A delivery person is standing near the door to hand them out. I ask for four. He looks at me for a moment, looks at the paper, then looks at me again and exclaims, "Hey, that's you in the article!"

I'm totally surprised that a stranger would recognize me. Turning red, I reply, "Yeah! That's why I want four copies. One for me, one for my dad, one for my grandmother, and one to flash at my best friend!"

"You're going to ruin me!" he answers, laughing.

He hands me the papers and wishes me a good day. I hurry and read the article. It's written in such an inspiring way, talking about Mael-a and me and our accomplishments. There's also a nice paragraph about the school elections, saying that it's time for our voices to be heard, with the things Samira and I want to change at our high school if we're elected. The journalist even included the slogan Samira came up with!

When I get to school, as usual, I feel like everyone's staring at me, except this time people are less subtle about it. People are straight-up pointing at me and whispering. I don't know if it's because of the news article or because my outfit is so breathtaking, but it's not unpleasant, even though it's a bit embarrassing.

I find Stephie in front of the locker. Before saying a word, I shove the paper under her nose. She exclaims, "Whoaaa! Too cool!"

"I took a copy to hang in our locker. Got scissors?"

Stephie hands me her pencil case.

"This has everything in it. Will you let me read it?"

I give her the paper, and she reads it quickly. In her opinion, it's very well done.

Once the article is cut out and taped to the locker door, just above the Stephel drawing, I tell my friend I have something else to show her. I dig through my backpack and pull out the envelope on which I've written "Liam." Stephie lets out a stifled cry and waves her hands around in excitement.

"That's why you're dressed so well today! Can I read it? Can I read it?"

"Oh, no way! It's private."

"Come on. I would have showed you if it were me."

I give in to her begging and pull the letter out of its envelope. Stephie snatches it and reads it, nodding her head.

"Mm-hmm, mm-hmm, mm-hmm, yeah.... Okay, it's good. Well done!"

Anxiously, I ask, "Do you think he'll say yes?"

"I hope so. In any case, I would!"

I wink at her and she blows me a kiss. I slip the letter back into its envelope and tuck it safely into my agenda.

"Do you know when you plan to give it to him?" Stephie asks.

"No. I'll wait for the right moment."

I sit on the floor with a copy of the paper to take a good photo and post it to Snapchat and Instagram.

Samira shows up and says hi. I ask her, "Did you see the article in the paper?"

"No, not yet. Do you talk about the school election in it?"

"In detail!"

I hand her a copy. After a moment, she jumps up and down and squeals with joy. "Amazing! With this, we're totally going to win! You're so good, Ciel."

"I taught them everything they know," Stephie says, teasing.

"Oh, really?"

"Can I keep it?" Samira asks, waving the newspaper.

"Ah, no! It's for my grandmother. But you can take a picture!"

I'm practically walking on clouds as I head toward my art classroom. It's harder than usual to concentrate in class, first because of the letter hidden in my agenda, and then because I can't help wondering who's read the article and what people will think of it.

In second period, during English class, it's worse. Mr. Lessard declares in front of the whole class, "Oh, Alessandra! Congratulations for your newspaper interview. You were a star in the teachers' room this morning!"

I smile and blush. It feels weird for a teacher to congratulate me in front of everyone like that. I barely dare to move during class, so I don't attract further attention. I've had my fill today, I think.

During the afternoon break, I run into Mael-a near the lockers while I'm chatting with Stephie. When they see me, they exclaim, "Ciel! Did you see the article? I thought it was excellent."

"Cool! Me too!"

We exchange a warm look. As Mael-a leaves, they say, "We'll see each other at the drop-in tomorrow!"

Stephie teases me: "Look at you, becoming friends with a fourth-year student!"

"We're not friends. It's more like a professional camaraderie. Like work colleagues."

"Like your dad, who's dating another college professor?"

"That's not official yet!"

"Oh, is that what you mean by 'professional camaraderie,' then?"

Stephie makes little kissing noises while batting her eyes in a suggestive way. She looks so ridiculous that I don't even deign to respond. She continues, "You know I'm teasing you. I know who your heart belongs to. Come to think of it, we have French next period, that would be a good time to give Liam your letter, no?"

"Are you crazy? In the middle of class?"

"Oops! Target approaching. Act natural."

I raise my eyes and see Liam coming toward us. My heart leaps in my chest.

He stops. "Hey, you two! How's it going?"

Stephie hurries to answer. "It's going really well, but I have to get to class early, I have questions for Mrs. Walter about the book we're supposed to read. Laaater!"

She trots off. I follow her with my eyes, bewildered. That was the least subtle exit I've ever seen in my life! She even turns around a bit further away to wink at me.

Preferring not to comment on what just happened, I say to Liam, "Things are hopping for me today. Did you see the newspaper article?"

"Not yet! So, is it good?"

"Yes. It's on the front page! I have it in my bag, I'll show it to you in class."

"Hmm, I was thinking of skipping class."

I frown, shocked. "Huh? Why? Do you have to go train?"

"No, I want to take a nap in the park. Do you want to come?"

I stare at Liam, trying to figure out if he's joking. "Are we allowed?"

"That depends if you consider 'allowed' from an ethical or legal point of view."

"What?"

"There is, of course, a rule that says we can't miss

class, but on the other hand, it's much too nice to stay indoors."

"What will happen if the teacher notices?"

"Worst case, we'll be expelled."

"I don't want to be expelled!" I say, frightened.

Liam laughs at my gullibility. "No, no. The worst that can happen is that we'll get detention. For me, that's a risk I'm prepared to take. Naps are good for your health. I used to take one every day when my mom was homeschooling me."

I remember that Liam told me he'd done all his elementary school at home. It must be hard for him to suddenly have such a strict schedule, on top of his training. I understand a little better why he wants to enjoy the nice weather.

"Okay. But…if I come, could they bar me from running in the school elections?"

"That would be antidemocratic. If it were to happen, I'd tell them I forced you to come."

The first bell rings and a pack of students fills the hallway, moving past me and Liam. I think for a moment.

"Let's do it. I'm coming!"

We exit by the student entrance, where latecomers (mostly the fourth- and fifth-year students who smoke between classes) create a certain chaos as they all rush indoors at the same time. Leaving school in the middle of the day is easier than I'd expected, even though I feel a bit like a secret agent on a mission.

There are two little parks near Simonne Monet-Chartrand, but we go a little further, just in case. We finally end up at Parc Maisonneuve, which is close to my place.

It's true that it's a nice day. It's as if fall decided to take a step back for a minute, tidy up the clouds it had left lying around, and turn up the heat. The park is full of people, which is surprising at this time! They've got their bikes, their running shoes, their portable barbecues; there's even a unicycle. Liam and I find a quiet area at the foot of a poplar tree, and stretch out on the grass to look at the clouds.

I ask him, "What do we do now?"

"Whatever we want. We relax."

The idea is foreign to me. I'm not used to relaxing. Even less so today, with the newspaper article, my love letter to Liam, the election…not counting that I'm in the process of breaking a school rule, which my dad would probably be mad about if he found out, and which might stay in my school file for life.

"Do you think it will prevent me from going to college, that I skipped a class?"

Liam points out all the people in the park. "See all these people? A good portion of them should surely be at a university class or at work. I don't think it'll bother anyone."

"Yeah," I say, unconvinced.

I contemplate the occasional cloud in the sky, thoughtful. Should I give him my letter now? But if he doesn't want to go out with me, it would ruin the moment…. I feel my phone vibrate in my pocket. I pull it out and look at the screen. Stephie's texting me.

> *Where are you?! The teacher marked you absent!*

I glance in Liam's direction. He's got his eyes closed and is breathing slowly. He seems about to fall asleep. I reply to Stephie:

> *I'm at the park with Liam. We decided to skip class.*

> *OMGGG! What's gotten into you?!* 😕 😕 😕

> *Don't tell the teacher!!!*

> *Of course not. But she seems to find it awfully suspicious that you both disappeared at the same time.*

> *...Sooo like you're alone with Liam? Interesting!* 😏

> It's not like we were doing much, anyway.

> *Well! Enjoy yourself!*

Stephie's right. I turn off my phone and shove it in my pocket. I say to Liam, "Can I put my head on you? The ground is too hard."

Without opening his eyes, he smiles and pats his belly to invite me over. I find a comfortable spot and settle in. With his warmth balancing out the little cool breeze that's blowing on us, I feel wonderful. My head moves up and down as he breathes, more and more slowly. Soon, I hear him snoring. It's a little less romantic, but just as adorable.

I'm about to fall asleep myself when my phone vibrates again. I look at the screen. It's my dad.

> *Where are you? The school left me a message, it seems you're not in class.*

Right away, I break out in a cold sweat all down my back. I should have known the school would tell him.

I have two choices: either I don't answer right away, to give me time to come up with a strategy...but my dad will surely think something has happened to me and will call the police and organize a search in the forest or something. Or I answer and tell him the truth.

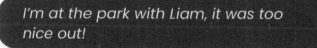

> I'm at the park with Liam, it was too nice out!

> OK. We'll have to talk about this.
> You almost gave me a heart attack.
> I'm going to call your school and tell
> them you haven't been carried off by
> a pack of wolves.

I put my phone back in my pocket, hoping very hard that my escapade won't cost me too much.

I rest my head against Liam's tummy once again. He's still snoring, and I end up falling asleep, too. When I open my eyes, the sun has dropped lower in the sky, and now we're in the shadows.

Stretching languorously, Liam extols the virtues of naps, but I interrupt him and tell him that the school told my dad I was absent.

Liam makes a contrite face. "Oops! I'm sorry. I hope you're not in trouble."

"I'll find out tonight, I imagine. But don't worry, I'm a big kid. I'm the one who decided to come with you." I try to seem assured and mature as I say this, but deep inside I'm worried about the moment I see my dad.

"You can still blame me as much as you like, I don't mind!"

"You're too kind."

"What should we do now?"

Without thinking about it, I open my backpack and take out my letter and hand it to him.

"Oh, look! There's my name on the envelope."

He smiles as he opens it. I hear the birds singing as he reads my few lines. I see his eyes moving from one word to the next. He laughs a bit. My heartbeat gets faster. When he finishes, he folds the letter back up and pulls me into a hug.

We stay like that for a long time, longer than my heart can handle not getting an answer. With a dry mouth, I pull away from his embrace and ask him, "So, does that mean yes?"

"It means I wanted to give you a hug."

"…Okay."

He lets out a little sigh. "I'm afraid I might not be the right person for you, Ciel. I don't really want to be part of a couple. I'm sorry."

I look at the ground disappointed. Tears blur my eyes. With a voice that shakes a little, I say, "So, it's a no."

"Not exactly. I really like being with you. I'm just saying we don't need to be a couple in order to be close." He takes my hand and continues. "Anyway, love is over-rated. If you want, you can be the person who's allowed to take naps on my stomach. Or the person whose hand I hold sometimes."

I frown, not sure I understand. "Well…that's like being a couple, though."

"It's like being a couple, except we have no expecta-tions of each other. No jealousy, either, because we stay friends. All the pros you list in your letter, without the cons!"

"So, we'd be like 'friends, plus?'"

"If you like."

I take a chance. "Can we…kiss?"

Liam seems surprised at my question. He stutters, "Uh…we can try!"

He leans toward me, and I close my eyes. As soon as our lips touch, his teeth bang against mine. He's clumsy. I realize that this is probably his first kiss, whereas I had a little practice with Eiríkur. After a few seconds, he starts laughing and pulls his face away from mine, before grabbing me and pulling me to the ground with him.

We roll in the grass, and we can't stop laughing. Deep inside, I'm a little disappointed about his response, but at the same time I'm relieved that it's all been said. And what we're doing here isn't bad, either.

♥ ♥ ♥

When I get home, I get a good talking-to from my father. He lectures me for quite some time about having cut class. He also makes me promise to tell him next time I feel like disappearing. Normally, I'd be on the verge of tears, but I keep my composure, doubtless because of what happened with Liam. I risk asking whether I can still go to the LGBT+ Center tomorrow. He agrees, barely, on the condition I come home by eight o'clock.

I call Stephie. When I tell her about Liam's reaction, she seems sad for me. I try to reassure her. "When you think about it, I don't really want to be part of a couple much either. Maybe I just need hugs!"

"I'll give you hugs, you'll see!"

"That's funny. Coming from you that sounds like both a threat and a promise."

15

The Detention from Hell

The next morning, at the beginning of my math class, Mrs. Campeau gets a call from the secretary on the intercom, wanting to see me in her office. Suddenly I'm very scared. The whole class turns to look at me, probably wondering what someone as adorable as me could possibly have done to deserve this. I smile at the teacher uncomfortably as I leave. She tells me to hurry up.

Not very reassured, I enter the secretary's office. Mr. Bégin greets me, twisting the ends of his moustache.

"Mr. Sousa!"

"I'm not a mister."

"Uh...yes, sorry, Miss."

"Not exactly a miss, either, but that's better than nothing."

"Hmm. Well, I spoke to your father yesterday. You decided to play hooky, it seems?"

When I'm stressed out, I make jokes. The words come out of my mouth before I can stop myself.

"I wasn't really playing anything. More like napping. Under a tree, to be specific, in the shade."

The secretary can't help but smile.

"'Playing hooky' is an expression. Do you know what it means?"

"That I skipped a class."

"That's right. I'm giving you detention tonight, at three-fifteen, in room B-204."

"I'll be there."

"Make sure to bring your agenda. The supervisor, Mrs. Trépanier, will put a note in there, you need to have your father sign it."

"Okay. Uh. Have a good day!"

I go back to math class, happy to have survived the meeting.

At lunch hour, I ask the others if anyone knows what people do in detention, so I can know how to prepare. Obviously, a model student like Stephie has no idea. Felicia says her big brother got a detention once, and it was just long and boring: sitting in silence, doing homework, things like that. I feel a little bit better hearing this.

I run into Liam in the hallway during the after-noon break. It's the first time I've seen him since we said good-bye in the park yesterday. I don't really know how to greet him. Should we kiss? Or hug? A high-five? What do people who are friends like us do when they pass in the hallway?

Liam opts to smile and wave at me. Liam smiling is already a lot, I have to say.

"Did you get a detention, too?"

"Yeah. But I still managed to amuse the secretary!"

"Well done. Shall we meet at your locker after class and go together?"

"Works for me!"

♥ ♥ ♥

The bell rings. I pick up my books and hurry to my locker. I get there at the same time as Stephie. Liam is already there, reading a comic book and leaning against the lockers.

"Hey, Stephie! Hey, Ciel. Ready to do penance? Bring something to keep busy with, or Mrs. Trépanier will make you copy pages from the dictionary."

"What? Isn't that kind of punishment against the law? And how do you know, anyway?"

"I'm a regular."

"Have fun," says Stephie. "Ciel, you'll have to tell me how it goes."

"Yeah, yeah."

I see her eyes are smiling, and she's observing us with an interested eye, Liam and me, doubtless expecting that we'll hold hands or walk more closely together. Anyway, when I leave with him, he does actually seem to be walking closer to me than usual.

Room B-204 is on the second floor. The halls are practically deserted. There are just scraps of paper on the floor and teachers wandering by, looking worn out. Our footsteps echo unpleasantly. When we enter the room, a woman of a certain age greets us and asks for our names, which she checks off on a list as she asks us to sit down.

"Do you have homework? If you have no work to do, I'll give you some."

Liam and I assure her we have everything we need. I rummage through my backpack and pull out the novel we have to read for French class. Liam, for his part, grabs his sketchbook and starts drawing lines in it. In dribs and drabs, students arrive after us and sit down in the classroom. They're all older than us. There are a lot of boys, most of them very burly and looking as though they've already had hard lives. Some of them joke with Mrs. Trépanier.

The detention begins in silence. After a moment, when everyone's settled in, the supervisor gets up and walks around between the desks. She tells a big fellow, who looks too old to be in fifth year, to put away his phone. He does, flexing his biceps, which are covered in tattoos. She clearly has great authority, and the students respect her, even though some of them are twice her size. I watch her out of the corner of my eye when she passes next to Liam. I'm afraid she'll disapprove of how he's using his time. She looks at what he's drawing, nods her head, and keeps walking. Phew!

When she finishes her rounds, Mrs. Trépanier leaves the room. The students in the back of the class start stirring and whispering. A boy sitting next to Liam leans over to see what he's drawing. He exclaims in a deep voice, "Hey, that's Boltron from *Ultra Robot Avengers* that you're drawing! Way cool. Can you draw Gigaoctet?"

"That's not my favorite character, but I can try."

Liam bends to the task under the boy's admiring gaze. The students at the back stand up from their chairs a bit to see his work.

"You're really good. What year are you in?" his neighbor asks.

"First year."

"Wow! I still draw stick figures."

Liam tears the page out of his sketchbook and hands it to him. The boy murmurs, "Thanks! I can't believe you did this without a model."

"You should put your drawings online, you'll be famous!" adds another boy.

Liam smiles. "Aw, they're just copies. I don't have a lot of imagination. Ciel, though, has a much greater chance of getting famous."

Eyes turn my way and I feel myself blush. What is Liam talking about!

As though it were no big deal, he continues, "You should follow their YouTube channel. It's called *Ciel Is Bored.*"

Telephones light up, the students look for my channel, and I hear my own phone vibrate, surely from new follower notifications. I don't know what to do with myself.

The big tattooed guy Mrs. Trépanier chided earlier asks me, "Hey, aren't you the one running for student council?"

I start to feel uncomfortable. How will these students react when they learn what committee I'm running for? But Liam is there and he looks at me benevolently. I feel my confidence re-emerge, so I respond, "Yeah, to represent the Gender and Sexuality Alliance with my friend Samira."

"I thought I'd seen your face somewhere," comments a guy with a nose ring who's sitting to my right. "It's great that you added the brown and black on the flag in your posters."

"Yeah, well, we felt it was important to show that we're going to work to make the group more diverse."

"You were also in the paper, eh?" the tattooed guy chimes back in. "Our social studies teacher read us the article yesterday."

I confirm with a smile. "Yep, that was me!"

"Listen, I'm not even sure if you're a boy or a girl, but I'll tell the guys from the school basketball team to vote for you and your friend!"

"And I'll tell the people in the wrestling club!" says the guy with the nose ring.

"Wow! Thanks, uh...."

At that moment, Mrs. Trépanier comes back, and calls for silence in the room. I'm still shocked at what just happened. I give Liam a hesitant smile, and he smiles back. Then I try to focus on my novel.

♥ ♥ ♥

"Thanks for advertising for me earlier, but next time, warn me first! I almost fainted when everyone turned around to look at me."

Liam and I leave the school and head toward the metro. The sun is low in the sky, and the air is much cooler.

"Ha ha! I'll try. Sorry, I have to hurry, my trainer is probably already mad that I'm late."

"Will I see you at the drop-in tonight?" I say hopefully.

"Ah, crap, I had totally forgotten that was this week! Listen, I'll have to see. I may end up finishing my training later because of the detention."

"That's okay. Text me if you're coming, and I'll come meet you at the station like last time!"

"You got it!"

When we say good-bye, we wave at each other, then we hug awkwardly and pat each other's shoulders. I go home to drop off my things and see how my YouTube channel is doing with all the new subscriptions from today. When Virgil comes back from his walk with Borki, I announce to him in a hollow voice, "I had a detention."

"How did it go?" he asks, worried.

"True torture. Mrs. Trépanier made us do sit-ups and push-ups while yelling at us until we cried."

"Whoa!" he exclaims, wide-eyed. Okay, so I'm exaggerating a bit, but it's in Virgil's best interest: I don't want him to turn into a rebel like his big sibling, as he calls me!

A glance at my phone tells me it's already time to leave. I still haven't heard from Liam. He must still be in the water. I take the metro to the LGBT+ Center. When I enter the room, I see everyone gathered around Mael-a, who's reading the article we're in out loud. They look up and smile when they see me.

"And here's the other star, just arriving now!"

A number of heads turn my way, and a girl exclaims, "Nice work!"

Mael-a finishes reading the article, and then Armand announces that he'll take care of having it laminated and posted on the wall. Then he says, "The buffet is ready, help yourselves!"

While we line up for the meal, a few people come to see me to talk about the article. The atmosphere is festive. Someone starts playing my YouTube videos on the room's computer, and very quickly, Dolores von Tragic becomes a star. They play the video on repeat, the short one where she's going nuts trying to get the hot broccoli out of her dress.

"That's your brother? You'll have to bring him here at some point!" comments a guy with neon green hair.

"Ha ha! He's too young, he's just nine!"

"I'm sure Armand can make an exception!"

We talk as we eat. The guy, whose name is Nathan, asks me questions about the school elections, as he'd like to have a Gender and Sexuality Alliance at his school. Once in a while, I can't help looking around the room, hoping to see Clementine and Sabrina. I'm sad they haven't come. I'm afraid it's because of what happened last time.

Mael-a speaks up and asks everyone to come closer. It's too cold to go outside, so we make the roundest circle we can with the space available. It ends up looking more like a kind of lumpy oval. I manage to find a spot on one of the sofas, squeezed between Nathan and the armrest. All of a sudden, I feel a hand tapping my head. I turn around and see Liam there, smiling at me. My heart leaps for joy.

"You! You were supposed to tell me so I could come meet you. I had lost hope!"

"I wanted to surprise you."

It's not easy to find space for him, as we're already squished together on the sofa. But Liam twists around enough to fit himself between the armrest and me, his legs halfway on top of mine. We laugh as he tries to get comfortable, putting his arm around my shoulders. Armand and Mael-a start speaking, but I'm barely listening. For once, I feel perfectly and completely happy.

16

Ode to Peanut Butter and Jam on Toast

On election day, I wake up as usual two minutes before my alarm rings. I feel shockingly confident, and fully on top of my game.

Yesterday, I spent nearly an hour on the phone reassuring Samira, who was more stressed out than ever. I have to say that, unlike us, Jérôme-Lou and Marine spent their last campaign day handing out tons of flyers, which got Samira worried about our ability to win. I ended up reminding her, "Don't worry! The whole basketball team and the wrestling club will be voting for us. And that's not counting the newspaper article, which will surely help. We've had more publicity than Jérôme-Lou and Marine could ever dream of!"

The morning goes by at breakneck speed. When we get to the cafeteria at lunch hour, we notice that a number of tables have been set up in the middle, covered with tons of decorated boxes. Student volunteers, supervised by teachers and Guy, the man in charge of student life, use their lists to make sure each student only votes once for each committee.

I insisted that Liam eat lunch at school today, so he could vote for me and Samira. After bolting our lunches, we get in line with the other girls. Jérôme-Lou approaches, shaking hands with everyone along the way.

Stephie sighs and rolls her eyes. "Get ready, we're about to be bothered!"

When he gets to us, Jérôme-Lou sticks out his hand to Stephie, saying to everyone, "Having a good day, I hope? Ha ha ha. Don't forget to vote for Jérôme-Lou!"

Stephie replies, "No, I don't think so. Samira and Ciel are also running for the Gender and Sexuality Alliance."

Samira adds, sarcastically, "Yeah, just saying, there's a pretty good chance we'll be voting for ourselves."

Jérôme-Lou answers distractedly, "Oh, no big deal, you can still vote for me! Ha ha ha."

He moves along without paying us any further attention.

Samira is mystified. "What did he mean by 'you can still vote for me?'"

Stephie adds, "What did he mean by 'ha ha ha?' There was nothing funny!"

We all crack up.

Liam reflects, "Maybe he's running for more than one committee…can you do that?"

"No idea."

While we wait to vote, I see the tattooed guy who was in detention with me and Liam. He's just come out of one of the two booths where you fill out the voting ballots. He notices me and calls out from afar, "I still don't know if you're a girl or a boy, but I voted for you and your friend!"

I give him a thumbs-up and yell over the crowd, "Cool! Thanks!"

As he moves off, Annabelle says indignantly, "Ciel, I'm so sorry! Some people just have no tact."

I shrug, amused. "Oh, it's okay. It's more funny than anything else."

"Speaking of people with no tact, look who's coming."

We turn and see Geoffrey, the guy who, with his little cafeteria performance, gave me and Samira the idea of running. He walks past without seeing us, too busy amusing his little group of friends by making fun of the people in line.

I murmur, "We'll see who has the last laugh!"

Our turn finally comes. Samira and I go up at the same time. We ask for ballots for the Gender and

Sexuality Alliance, and we disappear behind the booths. It's very weird to see my own name with Samira's on the little ballot, and to check the box next to them. My hand is shaking a bit. I fold the ballot like they told us to and go put it in the appropriate box in front of a student volunteer. When I find Samira again, we give each other a victory high five.

Liam, Stephie, Felicia, Annabelle, and Zoe also go up to vote. When he comes back to us, Liam says, "Guess what? I voted for you!"

"What a surprise!" replies Samira with a little smile. "Very pleased that you've placed your trust in us."

"Now, if you win, I hope you'll fight to have the cafeteria serve poutine once a week. That would encourage me to stay at school for lunch."

Felicia laughs, "Ha ha ha! You're too funny. You should eat lunch with us more often."

"Only if the cafeteria is serving poutine!"

I give Liam a friendly shove. "In your dreams!"

"When will we find out the results?" Stephie inquires.

Samira, who's still calming down, replies, "Tomorrow morning. They'll be posted on the board."

♥ ♥ ♥

Tonight, as if to underscore this special day, my dad invited Myriam and her daughter Leah for dinner. It's our first meal together in a good while that doesn't include apples, as our stock of fresh apples is starting to get low. However, we have enough frozen apple pies and preserves to last us the winter.

When she enters our apartment, Myriam congratulates me on the article that came out in the paper this week. "Anyway, your dad is so proud of you. He must have shown the article to every employee at the school!"

"Dad!"

My dad laughs as he chops vegetables with Virgil.

Myriam continues, "So, how did the elections end up going?"

"Actually, we voted today, and the results will be posted tomorrow morning."

"Do you think you'll win?"

"I don't know. Our opponent is pretty popular. And, he's the pet of the student life coordinator. But Samira and I got a lot of support."

Leah jumps into the conversation. "By the way, Ciel, I checked out your YouTube channel this week. It's cool."

Virgil interrupts. "Did you see the videos we made with Dolores von Tragic?"

"Ha ha ha! Yes, I saw them. You're pretty good. Dolores von Tragic is hilarious! Does she have an Instagram account?"

"Yes, I'll show you!" Virgil grabs Leah's phone. "There, you're following her. There aren't a lot of photos yet, but we'll add more, for sure."

"Do you want me to help you? I'm good at doing makeup!"

"Yessss!" cries Virgil.

As soon as we finish dinner, he runs off to put on his costume. Using my things, Leah does an incredible makeup job, matching it to his outfit. I'd like to ask her where and how she learned, but I don't dare, for fearing of coming across as an amateur. Instead, I direct Virgil on what poses to strike, and we take tons of photos with my phone. After a few clicks and lots of laughter, the new photos are online, and Virgil is as happy as if it was his birthday.

♥ ♥ ♥

Friday morning, unlike my usual habit, I wake up nearly a half hour before my alarm goes off. It's a new record! I can't get back to sleep—I'm too excited to see the school election results! I decide to text Stephie to kill some time.

> *Morning, sunshine!*

> *You still sleeping?*

> *I'm super nervous about the elections.*

> *Do you think Samira and I are gonna win?*

She finally answers:

> *Zzzz...*

> *Ah ha! I woke you up. One point for me!*

I watch YouTube videos until it's time to leave for school. As soon as I set foot in the building, I walk quickly to the agora. That's where the board is where they'll be posting the election results. There's a crowd in front of it. The students press in to read the names of the students elected to run the various committees. In the crush of bodies, I see Samira, who's also trying to find her way through. I join her. She gets to the list first, and reads out loud:

"Gender and Sexuality Alliance: Samira Mede and Alessandra/o Sousa!"

She lets out a scream of joy, and I fall into her arms.

"YESSS!"

We jump up and down on the spot, holding hands. The students around us watch us with amusement. I feel like fireworks are going off in my chest.

Samira cries out, "Let's go tell the others!"

"Of course, Madam President!"

As we head toward the first-year lockers, we pass by Jérôme-Lou and Marine, who are also beaming.

Jérôme-Lou says, "Hey, you two! Congratulations on your victory, ha ha ha. It's well deserved."

Samira replies, "Thanks! I'm sorry for you, though."

"Don't worry about us, we're celebrating our own success," says Marine happily.

"Oh yeah?" I reply, surprised.

"You're looking at the new president and vice-president of the student council!"

"You were running for both?!"

"That's right," says Jérôme-Lou. "Guy suggested it. They're similar tasks to those of the Alliance, but more important!"

Samira and I exchange a knowing look, before letting Marine and Jérôme-Lou savor their moment of glory.

"Well, in that case, congratulations!" I say.

They head off after adding, "We'll see you next week at student council!"

Samira is shocked by the news. But she quickly remembers she's now the president of the Alliance, and euphoria takes over once again. We skip to the locker where we find Stephie and announce our victory. She grabs me in a hug.

"I'm so proud of you. Congratulations!"

I'm really touched. She then gives Samira a big hug and congratulates her. Samira is teary-eyed. I smile and pat her on the back. I can't wait to get down to work together!

♥ ♥ ♥

For the day we're presenting our personal projects, Mr. Brazeau is wearing a black shirt with a bow tie that has little skulls printed on it. He definitely knows how to put on a show!

Once we're all sitting down, the teacher asks everyone if there are volunteers to present their project. A few students raise their hands. The first to speak is Siobhan, who's very excited to tell us about her new passion: macarons. She practiced for three weeks to be able to bake them to perfection. When she finishes her explanation, she brings out a huge clear container filled with colorful macarons. There's one for each student in the class, and one for Mr. Brazeau. Yum! I think she just made a lot of friends.

The presentations continue, and we learn about all sorts of topics: salt crystals, clocks (Frank apparently wasn't the only one to have that idea for his project), smoothies (no tasting this time), glue made with borax (nobody's very impressed; after all, we're not eight years old anymore), and stained glass (very pretty).

Just when Mr. Brazeau thinks there are no more volunteers, Frank raises his hand to go next. He hands Mr. Brazeau a USB key so he can put it in his laptop. The title of his personal project appears on the projector screen: "Garment-making." There are a few stifled laughs here and there, including from his best friend, Viktor.

A little nervous, Frank dives in. "At the beginning, I didn't think I'd make much, because I didn't know anything about sewing. So I took it one step at a time, and followed the instructions to the letter."

Frank documented everything: he took photos of every step, every piece of material, and every tool he used. He's so passionate that everyone starts paying attention.

"So this, obviously, is my girlfriend's sewing machine, because I don't have one. I wouldn't have put dolphin stickers on mine. This is when I was cutting the pattern pieces. Taken one by one, I know they look bizarre. They don't look like they're going to end up as shorts. Bit by bit, the garment starts to take shape."

Mr. Brazeau comments, "Wow! I'm impressed. Did it work?"

"Well, I had to sew some seams several times over, because I didn't understand how. But I think it worked pretty well, because...." He points to his jean shorts. "...I'm wearing them today!"

The whole class lets out a surprised cry. Nobody was expecting that, not even me. But when I look at Frank's shorts carefully, I can see that they are indeed made of the denim the store clerk gave him. Mr. Brazeau thanks him, and he goes back to his seat as people applaud.

I lean over to him and whisper, "I'm hiring you to make my prom dress!"

Frank laughs. Mr. Brazeau asks if there are any more volunteers, so I decide to go for it, inspired by Frank's success. I go up to the front and give my USB key to

Mr. Brazeau. "It's not a PowerPoint, it's just a video. You can play it when I give the signal."

"Sounds good! Go ahead."

"Hello, everyone! As some of you may know, I have my own YouTube channel, where I post the videos that I produce. That's why I wanted to do a project that was related to video-making. I chose to work on green screens, which let you change your backgrounds on the computer. I had to find a kind of lime green curtain, that, according to one of my friends, looks really ugly in my room."

A few people laugh. I summarize the various steps of my work, and conclude, "I want to show you the fruits of my labor: the new video I'm going to post tonight on my channel. It's called 'Ode to peanut butter and jam on toast.'"

I go turn out the light, then look at Mr. Brazeau, who starts the video. It's my old Barbie doll, who has seen better days—that's especially clear when you see her on the big screen. Behind her, there's a large-size parade of sliced bread, on which an enormous knife is spreading peanut butter, and then strawberry jam. While this is happening, we hear Stephie reciting a poem she invented the other day:

Sophie Labelle

Peanut butter and jam on toast,
How could I live without you?
You're the food I turn to most,
For breakfast, you're always true.

Some people look down on your taste,
They truly do not understand,
That salty and sweet, together placed,
The test of time will stand.

Salted peanut butter,
Or plain can be just right.
A rainbow of textures:
Crunchy, creamy, light.

The jams can also vary—
Peach, pear, kiwi, wow!
Strawberry, raspberry, blueberry,
And Nutella, we'll allow.

At the morning meal you most impress,
But I'd eat you for all three.
Ask what goes together best?
Peanut butter, jam, toast—and me.

When the poem is finished, the slices of bread disappear slowly in the video's background, and it fades to black. I turn on the lights again. Everyone starts laughing and clapping. One student whistles. I see Frank cracking up in his corner. Mr. Brazeau has tears in his eyes. I don't know if it's because he also wants to laugh, or if he was touched by Stephie's poetry!

I look around the class, proud of the success of my presentation. With a wink, I add, "If you want to know more, go subscribe to my channel, *Ciel Is Bored*!"

About the Author

SOPHIE LABELLE is an internationally renowned visual artist and author from the South Shore of Montréal, in French Canada. She is the transgender cartoonist behind *Assigned Male*, a webcomic about a group of queer and trans teenagers that has been running since 2014 and has touched millions of readers.